CHILTERNS
ILLUSTRATED
WALKS

Trevor Yorke

COUNTRYSIDE BOOKS
NEWBURY, BERKSHIRE

COUNTRYSIDE BOOKS
3 Catherine Road
Newbury, Berkshire

ISBN 1 85306 551 X

Designed by Graham Whiteman

Maps, photographs and illustrations
by the author

Produced through MRM Associates Ltd., Reading
Printed by J. W. Arrowsmith Ltd., Bristol

CONTENTS

AREA MAP SHOWING LOCATION OF THE WALKS

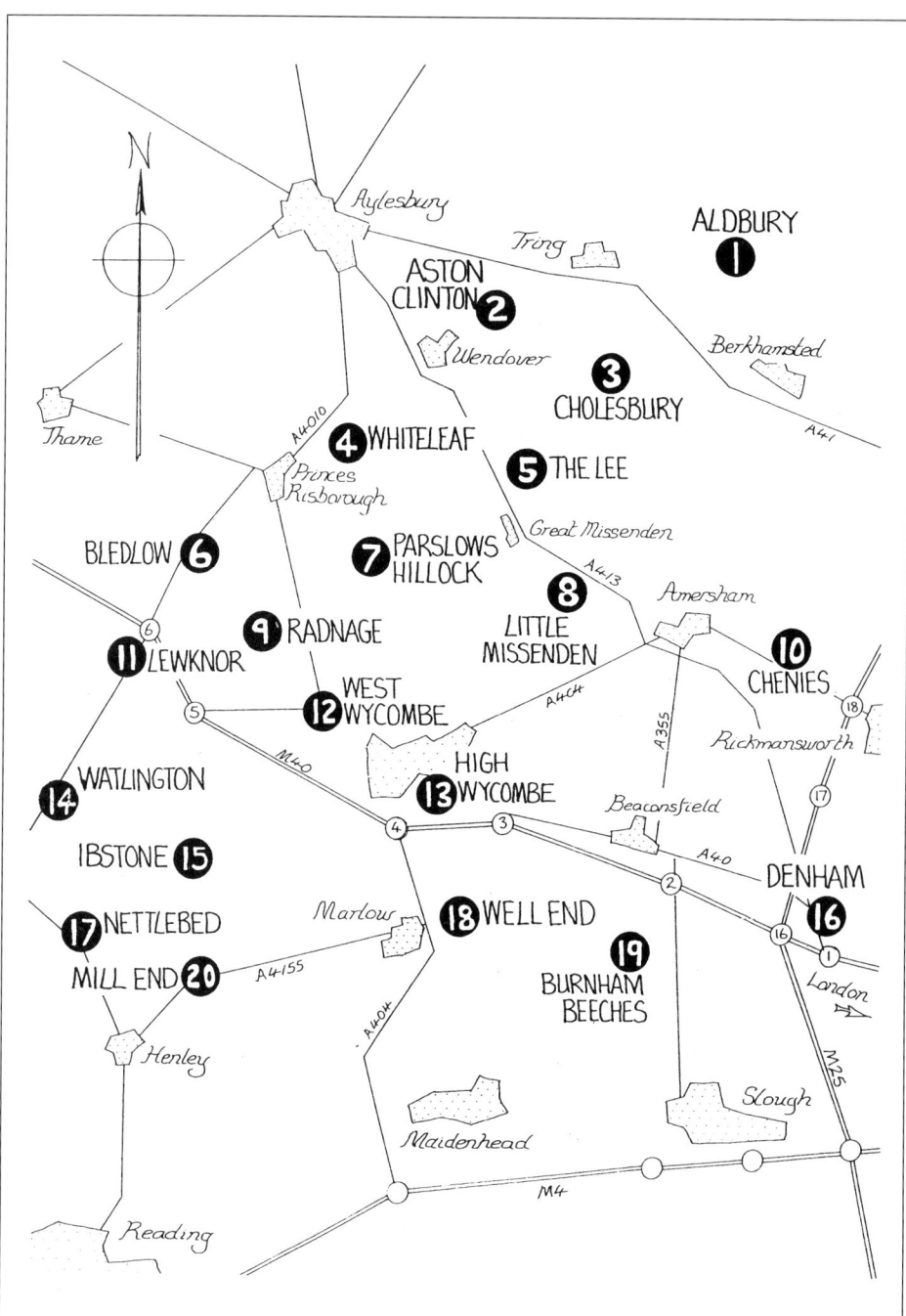

Walk

*To Dad for all his
invaluable help in
compiling this book.*

Publisher's Note

We hope that you obtain considerable enjoyment from this book; great care has been taken in its preparation. Although at the time of publication all routes followed public rights of way or permitted paths, diversion orders can be made and permissions withdrawn.

We cannot of course be held responsible for such diversion orders and any inaccuracies in the text which result from these or any other changes to the routes nor any damage which might result from walkers trespassing on private property. We are anxious though that all details covering the walks are kept up to date and would therefore welcome information from readers which would be relevant to future editions.

INTRODUCTION

Maps are wonderful things. Just a few lines and symbols on a page and the shape of the landscape takes form. Draw a cross next to a wavy line and most people would expect to see a church by a river. We use maps every day to find our way around town and country, and draw them ourselves when giving directions. We even hang antique maps on our walls as decoration. Yet despite all this familiarity, when it comes to walking books the maps tend to take second place behind masses of monotonous and ambiguous text.

With this fact in mind and by calling on my experience in surveying and illustration I set out to produce a book which uses maps rather than text to guide you around the walk.

To ensure that you successfully negotiate the walks, I have used strip maps whereby you follow the walk up or down the page in the direction of the arrows. This permits a larger scale and therefore allows me to show small details on the ground which can make the difference between taking the correct route or not. Also by imposing some approximate contours and shading I have given the map a third dimension.

Another advantage of this format is the extra space that can be dedicated to describing the places and features you pass on route. For instance did you know that it was the same clash of continents which raised the Alps 125 million years ago that formed the Chilterns? Or that most of the beech woods are man-made to supply the local furniture trade over the past 200 years? Facts like these in the text give a greater under-standing of the places the maps are guiding you through, although you may be happy just to admire the beautiful countryside.

The only thing left to decide was in which area to concentrate the walks. The fact that I have always lived near or in the Chilterns made them the obvious choice. The places and routes I have picked are my favourites from nearly twenty years of exploring these hills. I have tried to guide you through a wide variety of landscape. This includes the sometimes overlooked towns whose historic and attractive features are all too often hidden behind shop fronts.

Pubs and refreshments have been listed but no recommendations are made; it's all part of the fun of exploring! All the routes use public footpaths but please note that the parking areas marked may only be a road-side, so avoid blocking gates and driveways. For the walks I would recommend a good pair of boots although wellies will give protection against the worst of the elements. Although the maps are accurate for walking, they are not to scale and you may wish to carry with you the relevant OS maps for greater precision. The OS Explorer 2 Chiltern Hills North, and Explorer 3 Chiltern Hills South, cover the area featured as do the Landranger series 165 Aylesbury, and 175 Reading and Windsor. It is my hope that you find this format attractive and easier to follow than other books. More importantly I hope that you get enjoyment from exploring new places and discovering more about your old favourites.

Trevor Yorke

USING THE BOOK

STEP 1: With the map of the Chilterns shown on page 4 and a road atlas, find your way to the area. Then use the location map (example right) and its adjacent text to guide you to the parking place marked P.

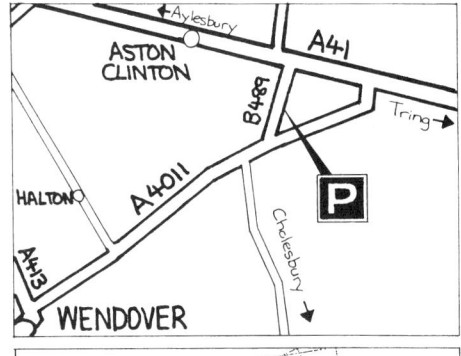

*Note that the parking may be no more than a convenient roadside, so please do not block any gate or access.

STEP 2: Overlying the location map is the route of the walk. The faint rectangles correspond to the areas of the strip maps and the map numbers are repeated in the top corner of each one.

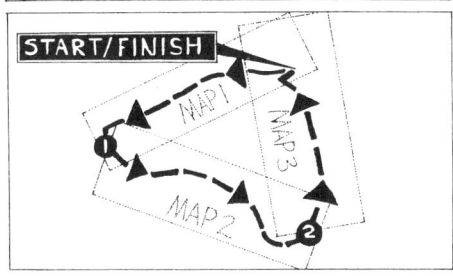

STEP 3: The walks will always start from the parking place. Turn to the first strip map and commence walking in the direction of the arrows. The faint lines and shaded areas are approximate contours. Dark areas are high ground, light are low.

STEP 4: When you reach the number in a black circle at the top of the page, turn to the next strip map and continue from the corresponding number on that page.

The number in the rectangle relates to that on the location map.

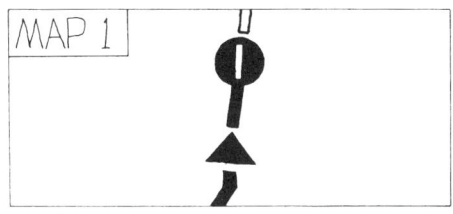

OTHER SYMBOLS

Rivers and Canals:		Buildings:	
Main Roads:		Churches:	
Other tarmacked roads:		Trees (Deciduous):	
Tracks:		Conifers and Pines:	
Paths:		Embankments and Mounds:	
Railways:		Cuttings and Pits:	
Hedges:		Stiles:	
Fences or Walls:		Gates:	

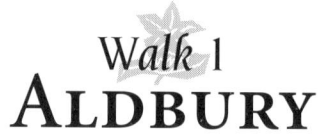

Walk 1
ALDBURY
Length 7 miles

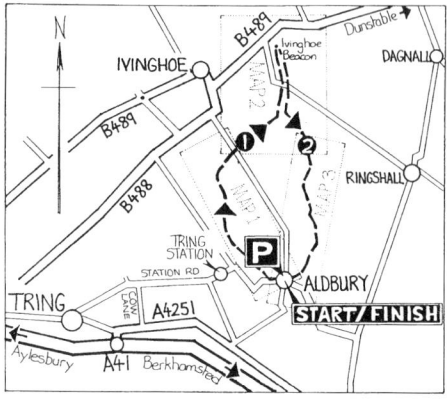

Aldbury

GETTING THERE: Take the A4251 turning to Berkhamsted off the A41 Tring bypass and at the roundabout below, go right (sign-posted to Aldbury). Almost immediately turn left up Cow Lane and then right at the next junction towards Tring station. Follow this road for 2 miles, over the railway and on into Aldbury.

Past the church on the left is the village green. Turn left here, up Stocks Lane, and park in front of the Greyhound inn.

INTRODUCTION: The best view in the Chilterns and its most photographed village lie at opposing ends of this dramatic walk. Between these points the ever-changing scenery switches from beech woodland to windswept grassland. Look out for the spectacular coombes and hills shaped by the ice ages and for fallow and muntjac deer which roam the Ashridge Estate; and you cannot fail to see the Bridgewater Monument.

ALDBURY: With a mix of rustic cottages, a green complete with pond and even a set of stocks, Aldbury composes a picture of an idyllic village. This has featured in many films and perhaps in order to discourage them the car park has been put slap bang in the middle!

The village has a number of older timber-framed cottages but it is the nearby Ashridge Estate which has had the greater influence with mostly Victorian brick houses, some featuring the Bridgewater emblem. The large timber and brick building to the west of the pond is the old Manor House and dates from the 17th century.

The church is most notable for its monuments, in particular those in the Pendley Chapel which were transferred here when the College of Bonhommes was suppressed in 1575. The building itself dates back in parts a further 300 years.

The most notable resident of Aldbury was the author Mrs Humphry Ward who lived at Stocks. Her first and most famous book was *Robert Elsmere* of 1888. Later she turned campaigner for the Anti-Suffrage League and became its first president.

GRIM'S DITCH: The route follows this ancient ditch and bank over Aldbury Nowers and Pitstone Hill. It could date as far back as the Iron Age although no one seems certain. See Walk 7 for more information.

IVINGHOE BEACON: The 'hoe' element of the name is Anglo-Saxon for 'a spur of land', most appropriate as you will see when you stand on top. The lack of trees makes for excellent views in all directions and attracts model aircraft and kite flyers as well as a steady procession of walkers. The hill also marks the starting point of the Ridgeway Path.

A small ditch you cross just before the top is one of the scant remains of an Iron Age hillfort which commanded the same view nearly 3,000 years ago. When it

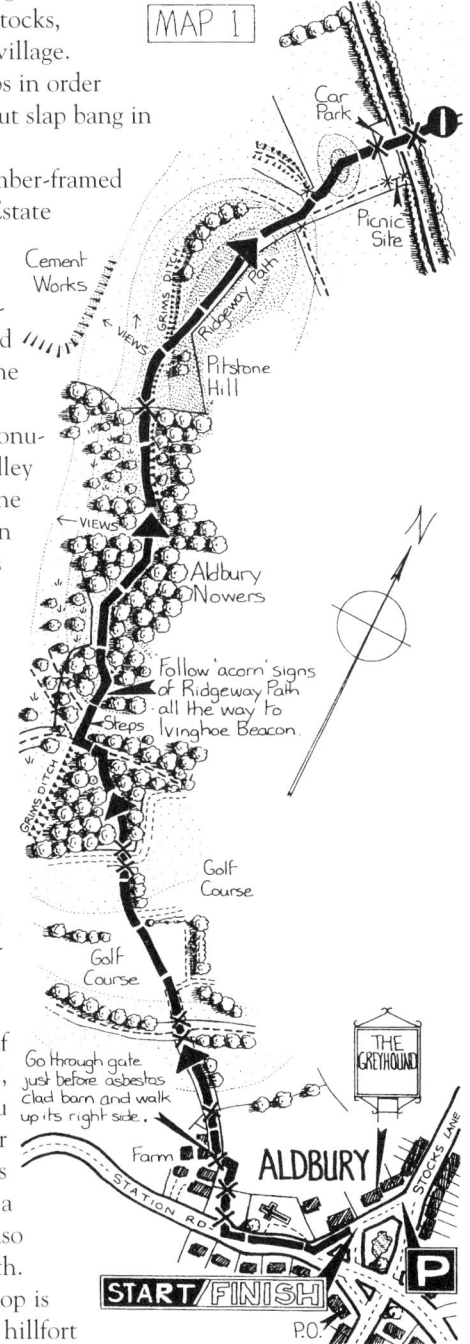

MAP 1

Car Park

Picnic Site

Cement Works

GRIM'S DITCH

Ridgeway Path

VIEWS

Pitstone Hill

VIEWS

Aldbury Nowers

Follow 'acorn' signs of Ridgeway Path - all the way to Ivinghoe Beacon.

Steps

GRIM'S DITCH

Golf Course

Golf Course

THE GREYHOUND

Go through gate just before asbestos clad barn and walk up its right side.

Farm

ALDBURY

STATION RD

STOCKS LANE

START/FINISH

P

P.O.

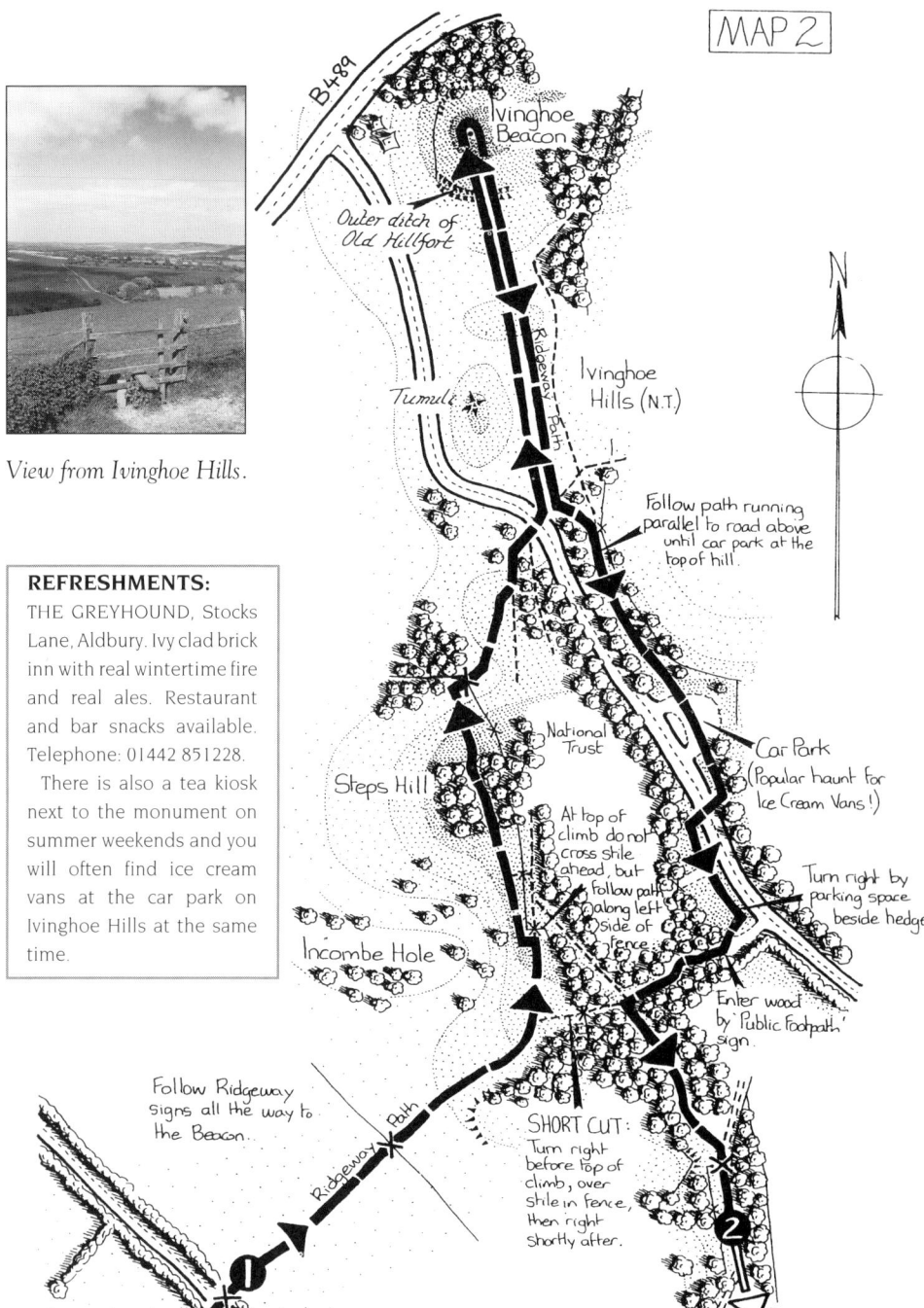

View from Ivinghoe Hills.

REFRESHMENTS:

THE GREYHOUND, Stocks Lane, Aldbury. Ivy clad brick inn with real wintertime fire and real ales. Restaurant and bar snacks available. Telephone: 01442 851228.

There is also a tea kiosk next to the monument on summer weekends and you will often find ice cream vans at the car park on Ivinghoe Hills at the same time.

MAP 2

B489

Ivinghoe Beacon

Outer ditch of Old Hillfort

Ridgeway Path

Ivinghoe Hills (N.T.)

Tumuli

Follow path running parallel to road above until car park at the top of hill.

National Trust

Car Park (Popular haunt for Ice Cream Vans!)

Steps Hill

At top of climb do not cross stile ahead, but follow path along left side of fence.

Turn right by parking space beside hedge.

Incombe Hole

Enter wood by 'Public Footpath' sign.

Follow Ridgeway signs all the way to the Beacon.

Ridgeway Path

SHORT CUT: Turn right before top of climb, over stile in fence, then right shortly after.

was excavated in 1963 it was shown to date from 800 BC making it the earliest discovered in England. There is also a burial tumulus on the smaller hill near the road.

If you look in the direction of the cement works you can see another first, this time the old post mill. Built in 1624 it is the earliest of its type in the country.

ASHRIDGE ESTATE: This National Trust property spreads over 4,000 acres along the hills from Ivinghoe Beacon to Aldbury. Apart from containing a diverse landscape of grass and woodland it is also home to deer, badgers, foxes, and the rare edible dormouse, while overhead you can see firecrests, redstarts, hawfinches, woodpeckers and nightingales.

ASHRIDGE HOUSE: Queen Elizabeth I lived in a previous house on this site until 1553 and it was also the College of Bonhommes until this was suppressed in 1575. James I sold it to Thomas Egerton who later became the 1st Duke of Bridgewater and it remained in this family until 1921. The present house was built by James Wyatt from 1808-1818 with a massive 1,000 ft façade and an entrance hall 100 ft high. The house is now a management college.

3RD DUKE OF BRIDGEWATER: The 3rd Duke, Francis Egerton, employed James Brindley to build him a canal linking his coal mines in Worsley to Manchester in 1761. The resulting navigation reduced the price of coal dramatically and helped start a transport revolution. With this in mind the huge granite monument was erected some 150 years ago to commemorate the 'Canal Duke'. If you have still got the energy you can climb its 172 steps! (Open April-October, Saturday-Thursday, 2-5 pm.)

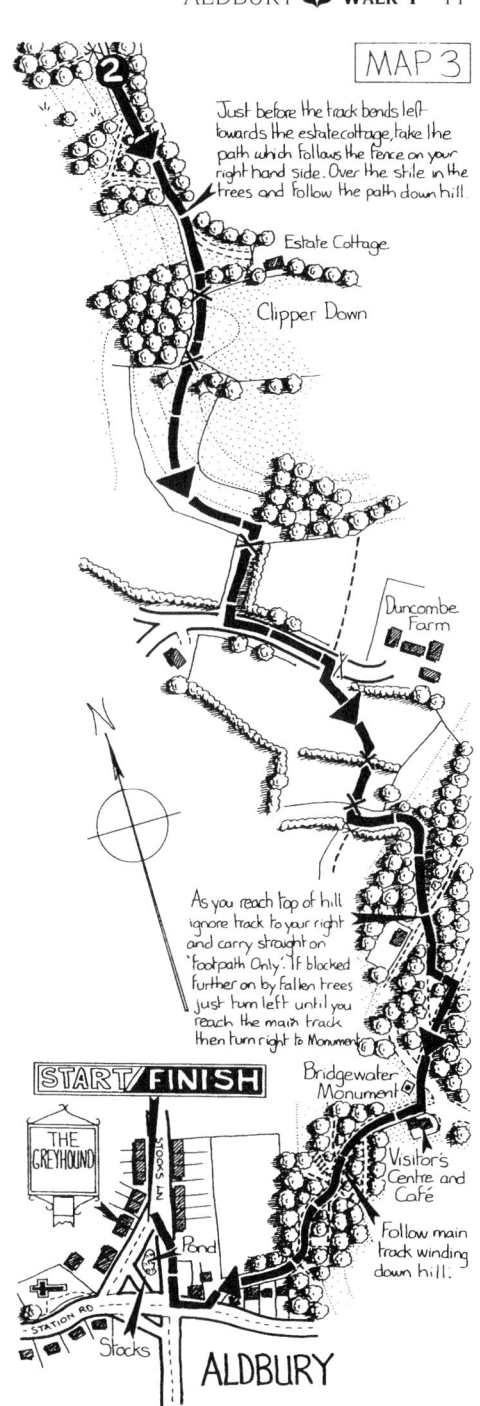

MAP 3

Just before the track bends left towards the estate cottage, take the path which follows the fence on your right hand side. Over the stile in the trees and follow the path down hill.

Estate Cottage

Clipper Down

Duncombe Farm

As you reach top of hill ignore track to your right and carry straight on 'footpath Only'. If blocked further on by fallen trees just turn left until you reach the main track then turn right to Monument

START/FINISH

Bridgewater Monument

THE GREYHOUND

STOCKS LN

Pond

Visitors Centre and Café

Follow main track winding down hill.

STATION RD

Stocks

ALDBURY

Walk 2
ASTON CLINTON
Length 4 miles

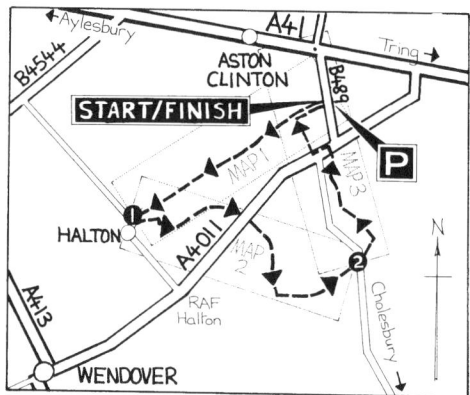

Halton Village

GETTING THERE: Aston Clinton is on the A41, halfway between Aylesbury and Tring. From the latter head towards the former and as you enter the village turn left up Stablebridge Road (the B489 to Wendover). Over the canal bridge there is a left turn into the car park.

INTRODUCTION: Despite crossing the Icknield Way and the nearby hillfort at Boddington Hill, this route takes you through a landscape created only in the past 200 years. It is dominated by the old estates of Aston Clinton Manor and Halton House and by the Wendover Arm of the Grand Union Canal which dissects the two. It is further influenced by the RAF training camp which you walk through. Mixed woodland and frequent views are the highlight.

WENDOVER ARM: The biggest problem faced by canal builders was water supply. This was especially acute on a summit section where locks falling away on either side would drain the canal. It is because of this that the Wendover Arm was built and more importantly survives today. When the Grand Junction Canal Company built their waterway in the 1790s from London to Birmingham they quickly realised that shortage of water on the Tring summit would be a problem. So they built a seven mile arm to Wendover which could not only transport goods but also collect water from springs to feed the main line. After another arm was built to Aylesbury the problem worsened and reservoirs had to be dug at Tringford with a beam engine to pump water up into the summit section.

Unfortunately the Wendover Arm suffered from leakage so much it was draining the main line rather than supplying it! Stop planks were inserted and later a lock built near Tring but in 1904 the section between Drayton Beauchamp and Tring was aban-

MAP 1

HALTON

Victorian estate houses

5' Mile post

Rothschild Bridge

Grandstand

RAF Sports Field

Airfield

VIEW →

Log Seat

NOTE:
Old horse drawn-boat rope mark in brick, near base of bridge. (Most have gone as the brickwork has been replaced.)

NOTE:
Slots in base of bridge for 'stop planks', to fit in if there is a leakage.

Yard

WENDOVER ARM

Log seat

VIEW →

Old Wharf
- now concrete lined due to leaking into old Manor House!

Old iron mile post ~ distance shown is from Bulbourne.

Green Park
Site of old Aston Clinton Manor.

STABLEBRIDGE ROAD

B489

P

START/FINISH

Rothschild Bridge

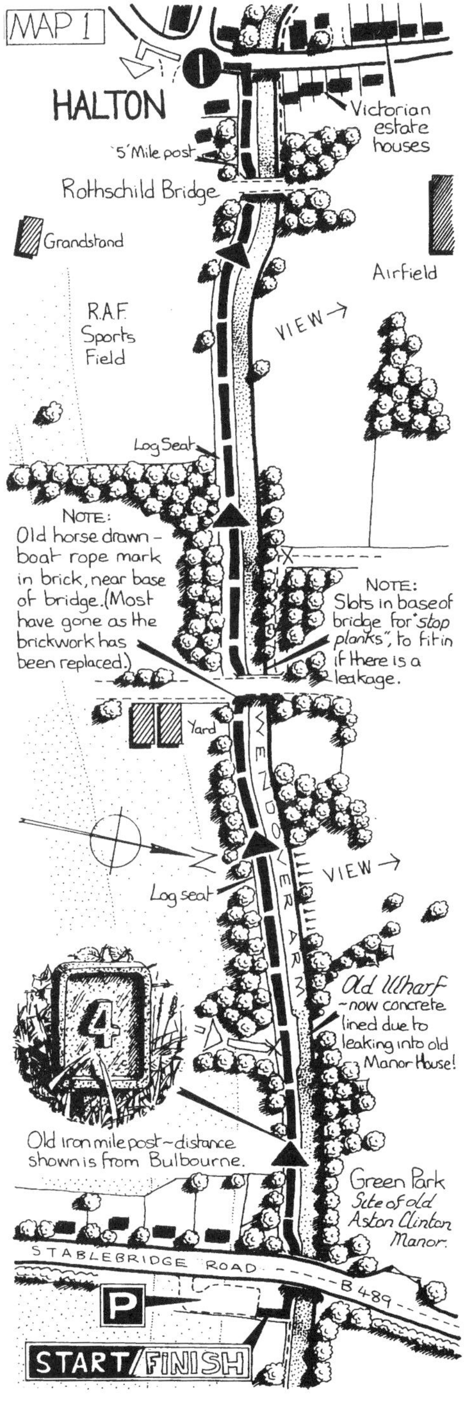

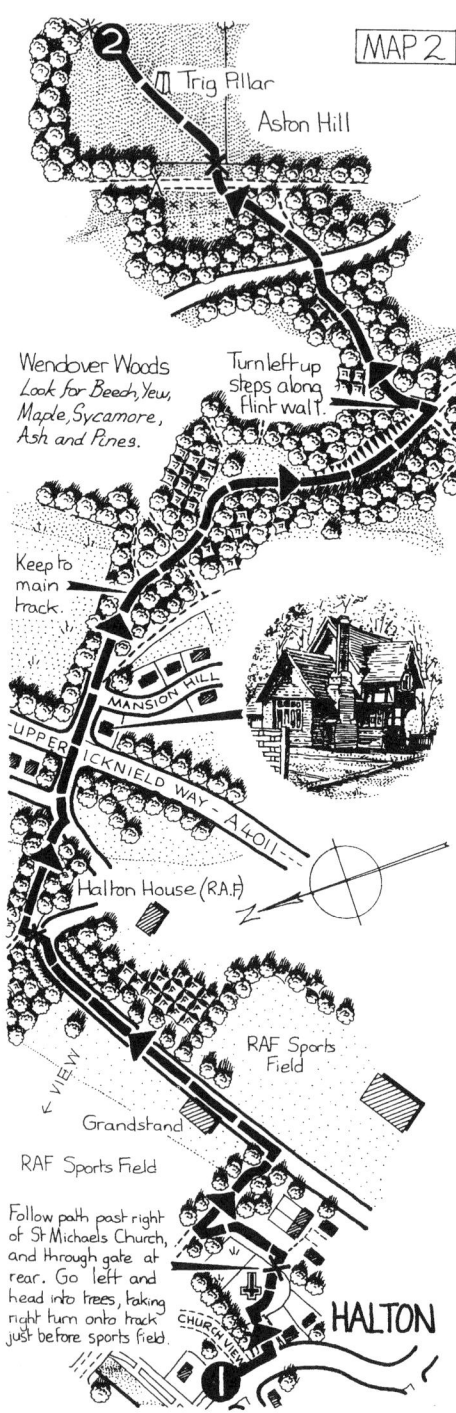

MAP 2

Trig Pillar

Aston Hill

Wendover Woods
Look for Beech, Yew,
Maple, Sycamore,
Ash and Pines.

Turn left up
steps along
flint wall.

Keep to
main
track.

MANSION HILL

UPPER ICKNIELD WAY - A4011

Halton House (R.A.F)

RAF Sports
Field

VIEW

Grandstand

RAF Sports Field

Follow path past right
of St Michaels Church,
and through gate at
rear. Go left and
head into trees, taking
right turn onto track
just before sports field.

CHURCH VIEW

HALTON

doned and drained. The precious water supply from Wendover was diverted into Wilstone Reservoir from which it could be pumped into the summit section.

The canal you are now walking along is lifeless and only half full but it has survived and has created a peaceful haven enclosed in trees with occasional glimpses of the Vale beyond. The Old Wharf at Green Park was used to transport goods to Aston Clinton House while the decorative Rothschild Bridge is a reminder of the owners of Halton House.

HALTON: A cluster of old cottages around the canal rather lost in the RAF training camp which surrounds it. A few houses are pre 1800 (look for the undulating roof lines on the two nearest the canal) but the majority are Victorian, built for workers on the Rothschilds' estate. Notice the decorated panels which have illustrations of the seasons and rural crafts on them, and the Rothschilds' motto: 'Concordia, Industria, Integritas'.

ST MICHAEL'S CHURCH: Built in 1813 the notable feature of this compact, tidy building is the exterior. Blocks of quartz-like grey masonry with small flints inserted in the mortar. It looks at first glance that it's been nailed together!

HALTON HOUSE: The Rothschilds bought the Halton Estate in the 1850s but it was Alfred de Rothschild who had the present house built in 1884. The French chateau style is similar to Waddesdon (another Rothschild mansion) and was used for some scenes in the film *Evita*. Mr Alfred, as he was known, is said to have driven round his estate in a carriage pulled by zebras and he had a circus of animals in a field near the mansion. He held agricultural shows and sometimes conducted his own orchestra while visitors surveyed his prize vegetables! After his death in 1918 the grounds became the RAF training camp and the house the officers' mess. (Please keep to the signed footpath through the RAF property.) The woods you walk through on the climb up to Aston Hill are littered with yews and the odd bit of flint walling – reminders that these were part of the Halton Estate.

ASTON HILL: In 1914 the ascent up Aston Hill was a renowned motoring venue. One driver, Lionel Martin, had such success in a retuned Singer that when he registered his first car in the following year it was called 'Aston Martin'! Fans of this famous motoring name have erected a pillar next to the car park on top of the hill which tells this story in more detail.

The walk down the hill follows an old holloway which would have been the original route down Aston Hill. Its course would have taken it along the present road from the golf club down to the Upper Icknield Way, across this and then through the strip of woodland through which you walk to the Wendover Arm. Take care descending the hill as it is crossed by numerous mountain bike tracks.

REFRESHMENTS:
THE RISING SUN, Aston Clinton. Lively pub with beer garden and restaurant. Open 11 am to 11 pm. Telephone: 01296 630399.
THE CROWS NEST, Tring. Beefeater pub with bar snacks and garden (excellent views). Open 11 am to 11 pm. Telephone: 01442 824819.

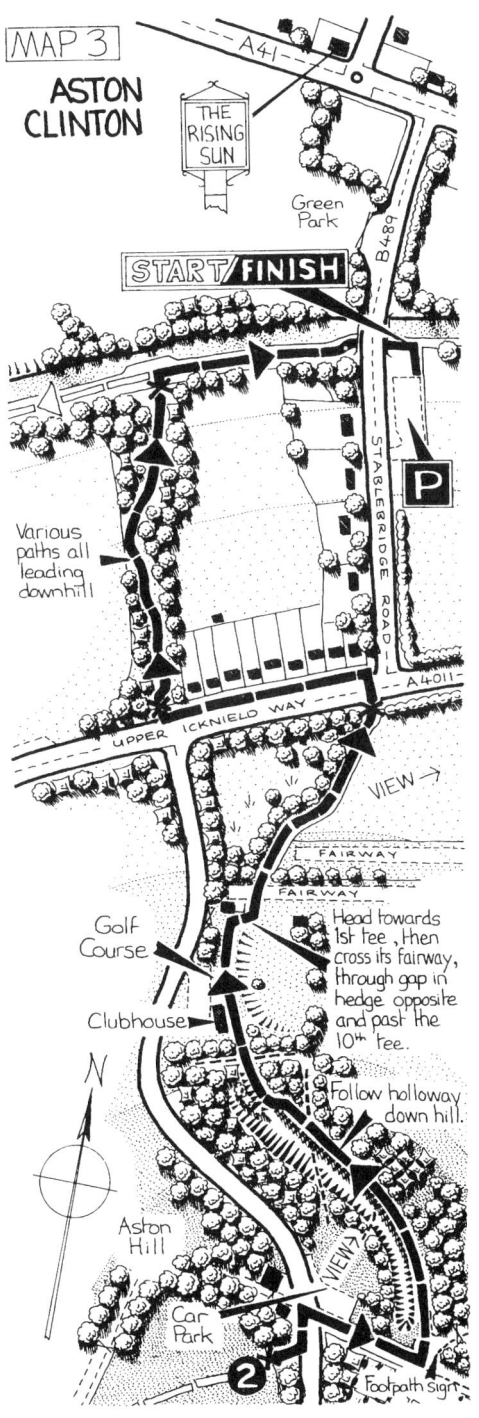

Walk 3
CHOLESBURY
Length 4 miles

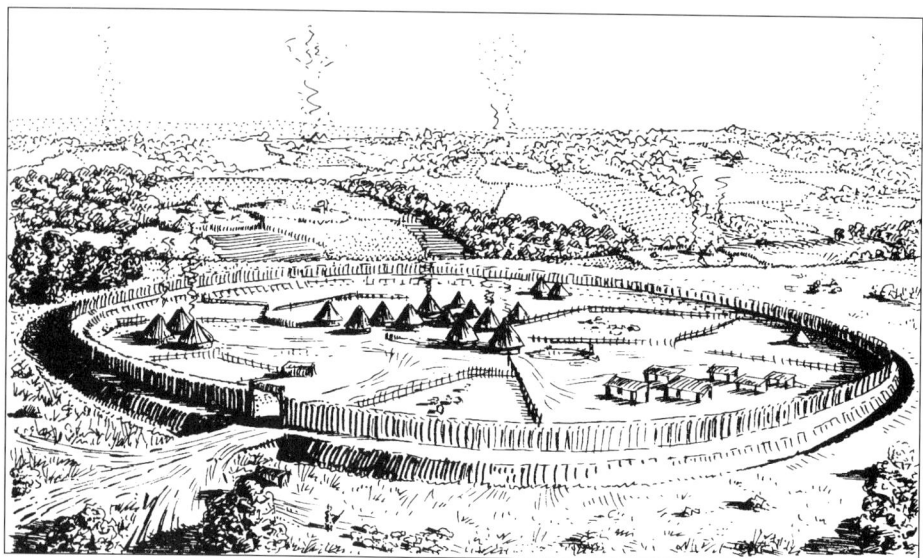

Cholesbury hillfort

GETTING THERE: From Tring – take the A41 towards Aylesbury and then turn left up the A4011 to Wendover. After ½ mile, at the top of the hill turn left towards Chesham. Follow the road for 4 miles through St Leonards and Cholesbury and park on the left at the end of the common by the Jubilee Stone.

From Chesham – take the A416 north out of the town and when the main road turns sharp right uphill, carry straight on along the minor road. Follow the road for 3 miles, through Hawridge, until just past the Full Moon turn right and park on the common next to the Jubilee Stone.

INTRODUCTION: Hidden behind a ring of trees is the huge hillfort of Cholesbury, its deep cuttings testament to the effort it took

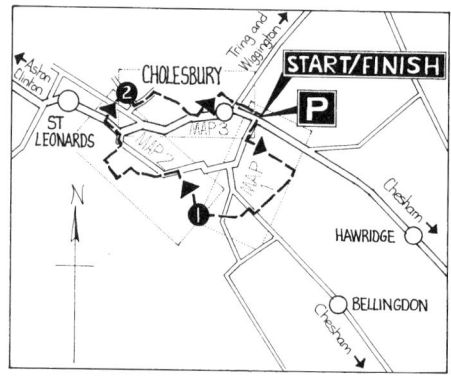

Iron Age man to dig it out by hand. The walk takes you through this piece of history and then round a mix of scenery on this Chiltern plateau including the Old Dundridge Manor and past one of the last working brickworks in the area.

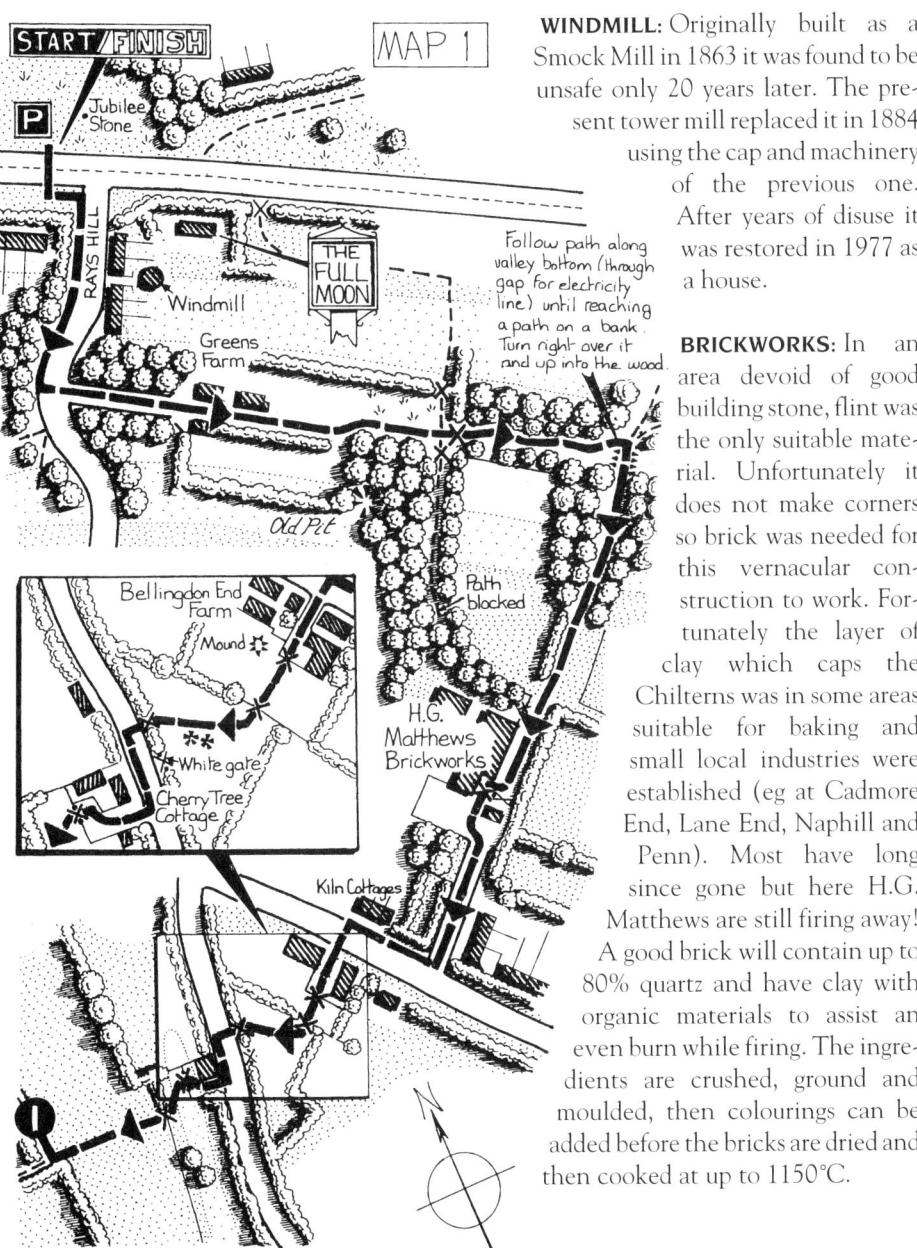

MAP 1

Follow path along valley bottom (through gap for electricity line) until reaching a path on a bank. Turn right over it and up into the wood.

WINDMILL: Originally built as a Smock Mill in 1863 it was found to be unsafe only 20 years later. The present tower mill replaced it in 1884 using the cap and machinery of the previous one. After years of disuse it was restored in 1977 as a house.

BRICKWORKS: In an area devoid of good building stone, flint was the only suitable material. Unfortunately it does not make corners so brick was needed for this vernacular construction to work. Fortunately the layer of clay which caps the Chilterns was in some areas suitable for baking and small local industries were established (eg at Cadmore End, Lane End, Naphill and Penn). Most have long since gone but here H.G. Matthews are still firing away! A good brick will contain up to 80% quartz and have clay with organic materials to assist an even burn while firing. The ingredients are crushed, ground and moulded, then colourings can be added before the bricks are dried and then cooked at up to 1150°C.

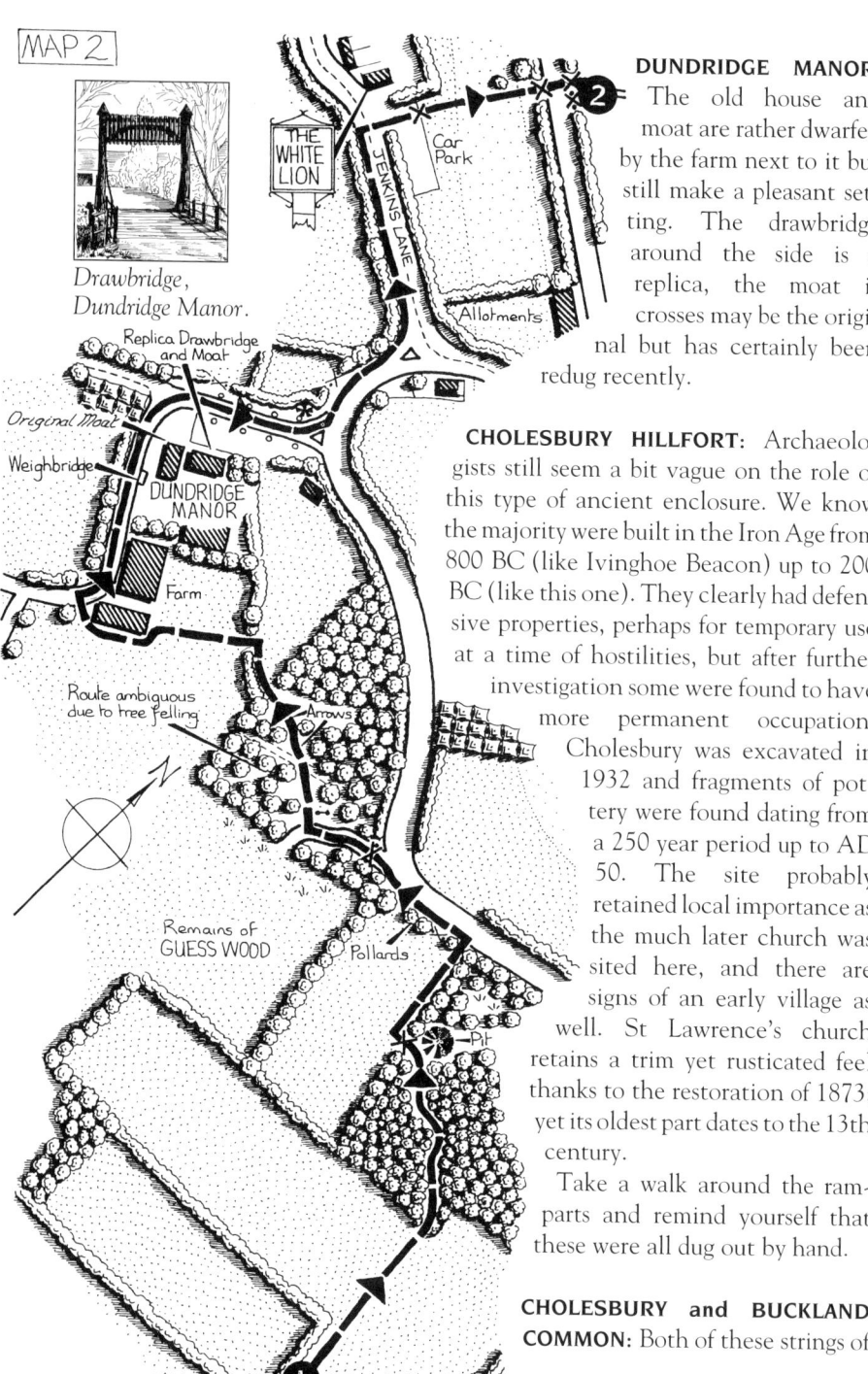

MAP 2

Drawbridge,
Dundridge Manor.

DUNDRIDGE MANOR:
The old house and
moat are rather dwarfed
by the farm next to it but
still make a pleasant setting. The drawbridge
around the side is a
replica, the moat it
crosses may be the origi-
nal but has certainly been
redug recently.

CHOLESBURY HILLFORT: Archaeologists still seem a bit vague on the role of
this type of ancient enclosure. We know
the majority were built in the Iron Age from
800 BC (like Ivinghoe Beacon) up to 200
BC (like this one). They clearly had defen-
sive properties, perhaps for temporary use
at a time of hostilities, but after further
investigation some were found to have
more permanent occupation.
Cholesbury was excavated in
1932 and fragments of pottery were found dating from
a 250 year period up to AD
50. The site probably
retained local importance as
the much later church was
sited here, and there are
signs of an early village as
well. St Lawrence's church
retains a trim yet rusticated feel
thanks to the restoration of 1873;
yet its oldest part dates to the 13th
century.
   Take a walk around the ramparts and remind yourself that
these were all dug out by hand.

**CHOLESBURY and BUCKLAND
COMMON:** Both of these strings of

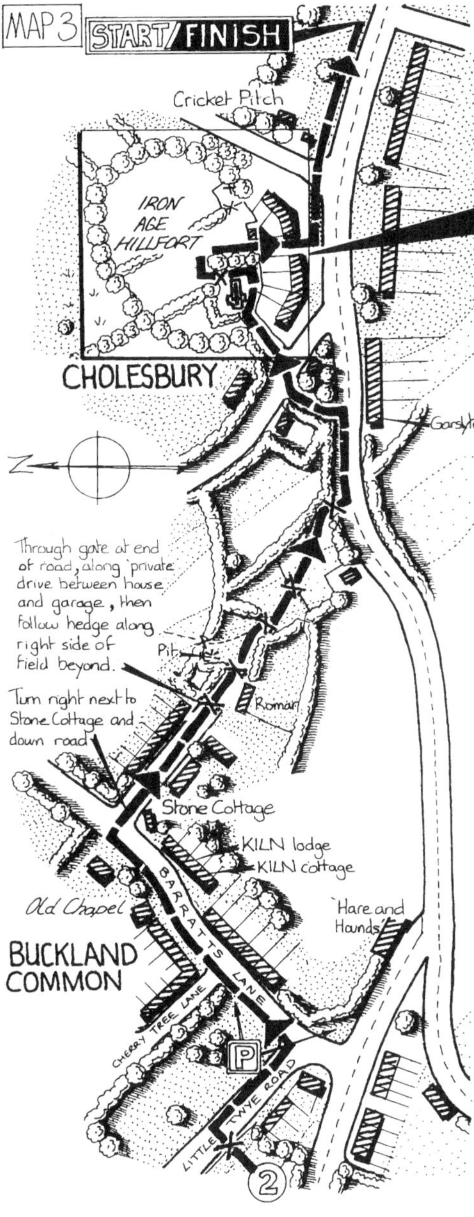

MAP 3 START/FINISH

Cricket Pitch

IRON
AGE
HILLFORT

CHOLESBURY

Garslye

N

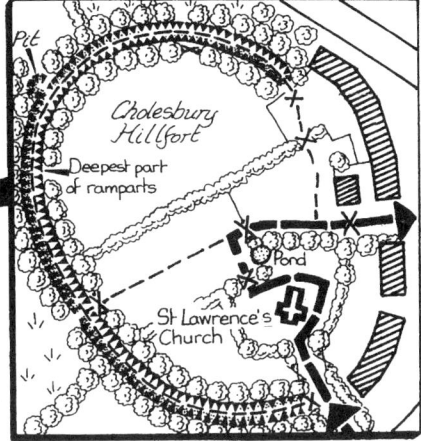

Pit

Cholesbury
Hillfort

Deepest part
of ramparts

St Lawrence's
Church

Pond

Through gate at end
of road, along 'private'
drive between house
and garage, then
follow hedge along
right side of
field beyond.

Pit

Turn right next to
Stone Cottage and
down road

Roman

Stone Cottage

KILN lodge
KILN cottage

Old Chapel

Hare and
Hounds

BUCKLAND
COMMON

CHERRY TREE LANE

BARRAT'S LANE

P

LITTLE TWYE ROAD

2

REFRESHMENTS:

THE WHITE LION, Jenkins Lane. Attractive pub dating back nearly 300 years and claiming to be the highest pub in the Chilterns. Open 11 am to 2.30 pm and 6 pm to 11 pm; no meals Sunday evening. Telephone: 01494 758387.

THE FULL MOON. Another excellent pub which dates back to the 17th century. Open 12 noon to 3 pm and 6 pm to 11 pm; no meals Sunday evening. Telephone 01494 758262.

Stone Cottage, Buckland Common.

cottages started as summer grazing land for parishes in the Vale below; Cholesbury with Drayton Beauchamp and the latter with Buckland. Although there is no record of brickmaking until 1717 it almost certainly existed previously; a locally produced brick in the earlier Dundridge Manor has a pheasant's foot imprinted in it from when it had been left out to dry. The numerous 'Kiln Cottages' hark back to this important trade.

Walk 4
WHITELEAF
Length 6 miles

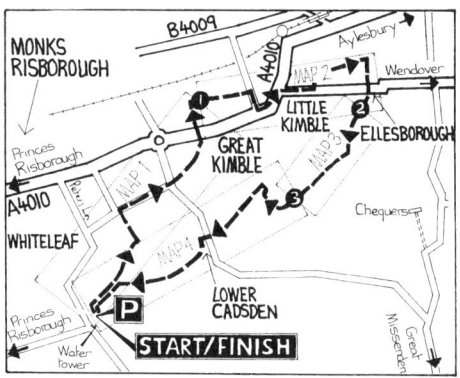

Whiteleaf

GETTING THERE: From Princes Risborough town centre head out on the A4010 to Aylesbury. After entering Monks Risborough take a right turn up Peters Lane signposted to 'Whiteleaf and Hampden'. After ½ mile the road bends right then left up a steep hill and as it levels off at the top there is a left turn into the car park (next to a water tower hidden in the trees).

To start the walk, head out of the car park in the direction you came and turn right upon reaching the path which runs along the edge of the escarpment.

INTRODUCTION: If ever I want to introduce a friend to the Chilterns this is the walk I take them on. It's packed with all the features which attract people to the hills: dramatic views, picturesque villages, and mighty beech woodland. You start with the mysterious white cross and barrows, then

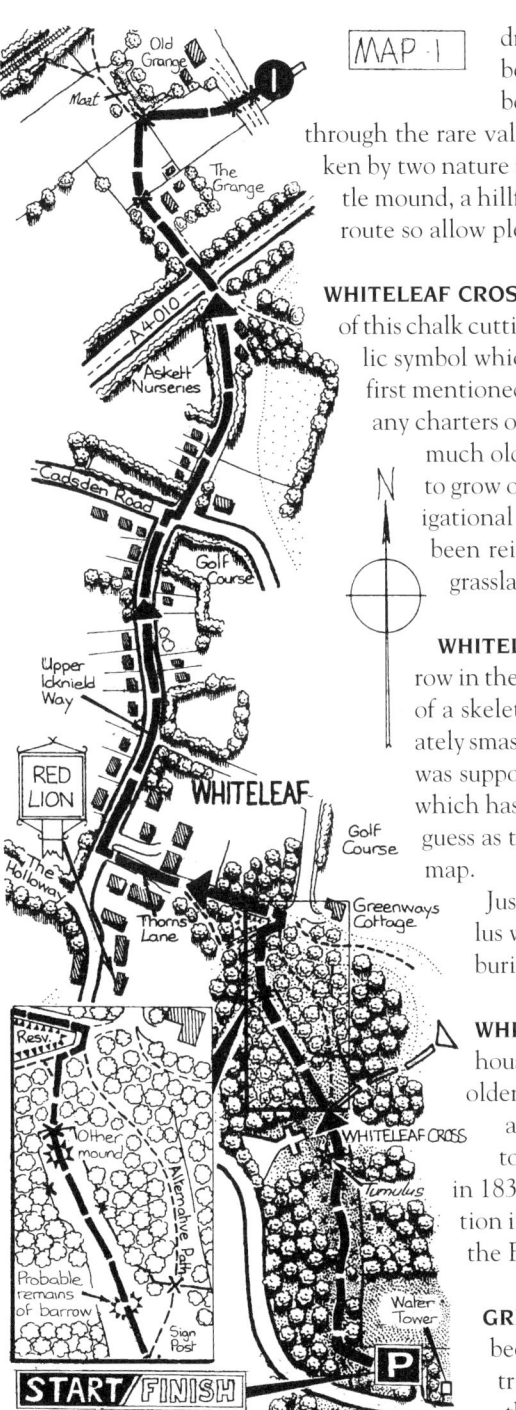

drop into the open pastures of the Vale before climbing past the pinnacle of Ellesborough church. Up over Beacon Hill and through the rare valley full of box and into beech woods broken by two nature reserves. You will come across an old Castle mound, a hillfort, three churches and three pubs on the route so allow plenty of time to take it all in.

WHITELEAF CROSS: Numerous stories surround the origins of this chalk cutting, including that it was previously a phallic symbol which the local monks recut into a cross! It is first mentioned in the 1700s but as it does not appear on any charters or boundaries before this it is unlikely to be much older. In the last war foliage was encouraged to grow over it so that it could not be used as a navigational aid by enemy aircraft. Today sheep have been reintroduced to return the slopes to natural grassland.

WHITELEAF BARROW: The only Neolithic barrow in the area was excavated in 1930 revealing part of a skeleton and 57 pots. These had been deliberately smashed as part of the burial ritual! The mound was supported by a timber chamber the removal of which has left little of the barrow, in fact I can only guess as to where it is and have marked this on the map.

Just before the cross is a more definite tumulus which marks a later, probably Bronze Age, burial.

WHITELEAF: A string of mainly modern houses along the Upper Icknield Way. The older and quite attractively set buildings are around the Red Lion pub. Numerous skeletons were found in a field above the village in 1830. As they were lain in an east-west direction it was a Christian burial, possibly caused by the Black Death!

GREAT KIMBLE: This ancient site must have been among the earliest settled in the district, being next to the Icknield Way and that rare commodity of water. The church

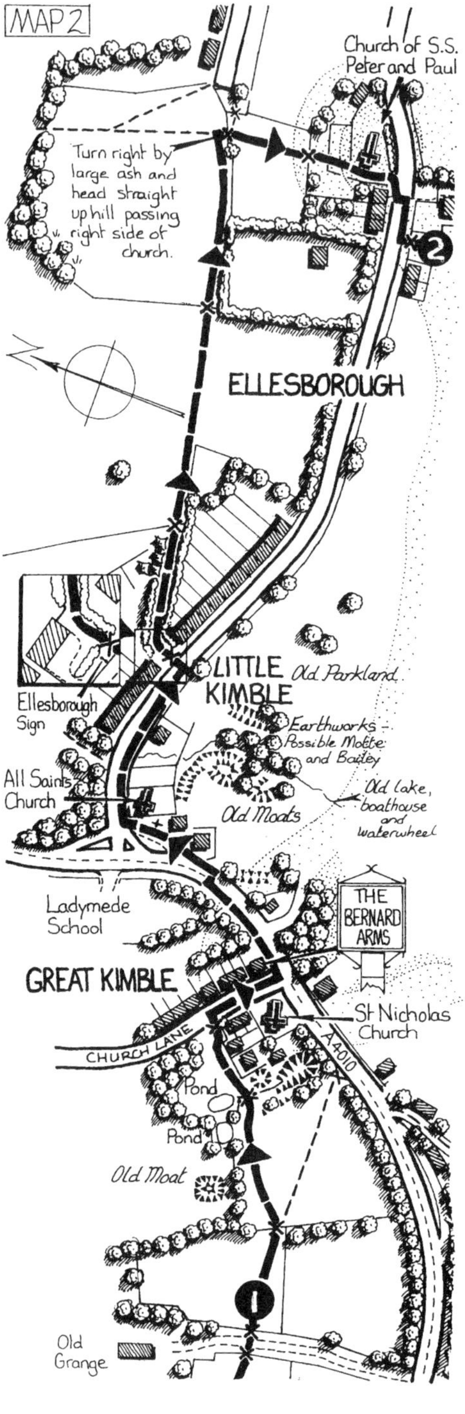

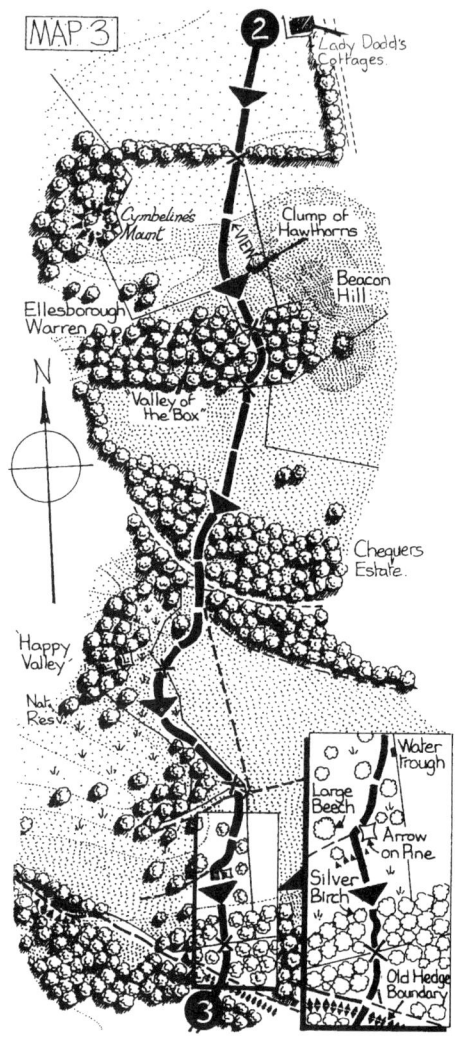

dates back to the 13th century and is famous for being the meeting place where John Hampden made his celebrated protest against the payment of Ship Money (see Walk 7). The deep gorge behind the church is another spring like the Lyde at Bledlow while in the fields between here and The Grange are a series of earthworks and ponds. There is a moat, still with some water, around The Grange and another in the field next door, while I have also found a mention of 'old intrenchments', possibly from the Civil War. Today the walk up Church Lane is picturesque and peaceful only to be shattered by the A4010 at the top!

LITTLE KIMBLE: While constructing the new turnpike road in the early 1800s workmen came across a 'tessellated pavement', Roman in origin, along with flint foundations. In 1855 archaeologists revealed more foundations, tiles, bones and stucco and concluded that Little Kimble was the site of at least a villa with possible other associated buildings. In the fields behind the church are further earthworks including a possible motte and bailey castle and a lake which used to have a boathouse and waterwheel.

The church is of special note despite its plain exterior. Inside wall paintings were discovered dating from the early 14th century. Most of our medieval churches had colourfully decorated interiors like this; it was only in the reformed 16th and 17th centuries that they were whitewashed to give us a mistaken image of a traditional interior. There are also 'Chertsey' style floor tiles on the chancel floor which date from the 13th century; similar ones, along with the locally made Penn tiles, can be found in the British Museum.

ELLESBOROUGH: Picturesque set of thatched cottages under the dominating church. This is famous for its guest list which includes Prime Ministers and Presidents as it is the parish church for nearby Chequers. Opposite are Lady Dodd's Cottages constructed 250 years ago as a dwelling for the local poor and still bearing the board of strict house rules.

Great Kimble

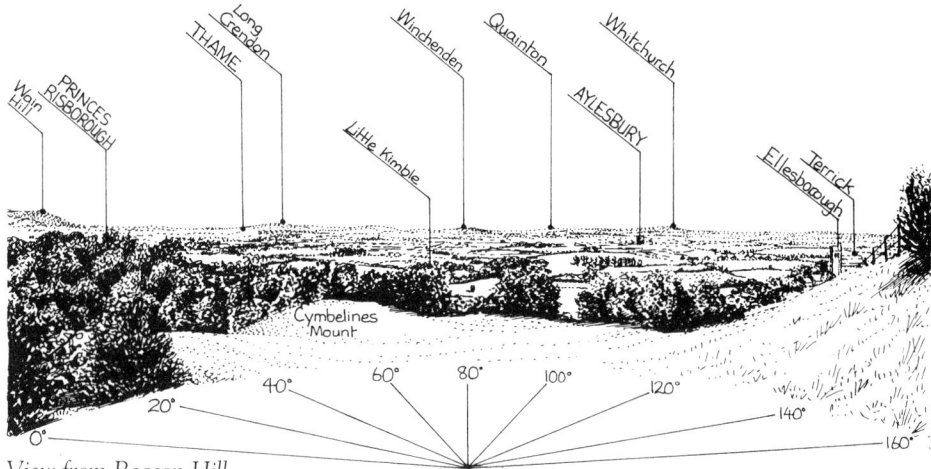

The view from Whiteleaf Cross

CYMBELINE'S MOUNT: An old motte and bailey castle, today covered in undergrowth and fenced off to be almost invisible. It would have dated from the 11th or 12th century and would have had a wooden tower and pallisade (see drawing in Walk 8).

BEACON HILL: This grassy knoll is part of the Chequers Estate so the best view (see drawing) is from a clump of hawthorn on

View from Beacon Hill

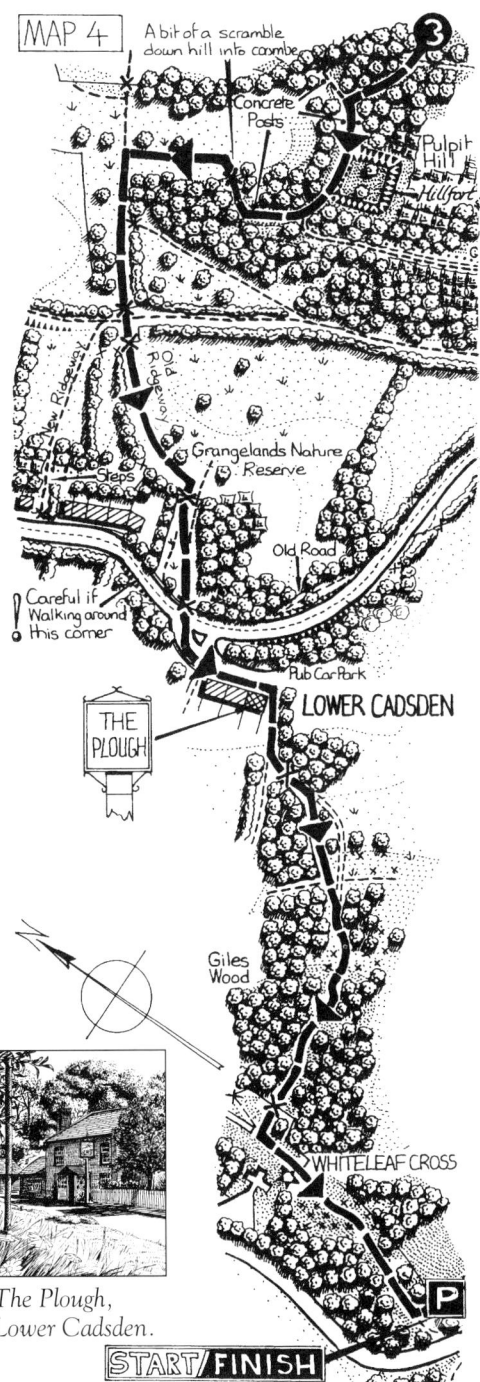

MAP 4 | A bit of a scramble down hill into coombe

Concrete Posts

Pulpit Hill

Hillfort

Old Ridgeway

Grangelands Nature Reserve

Steps

Old Road

Careful if Walking around this corner

Pub Car Park

LOWER CADSDEN

THE PLOUGH

Giles Wood

WHITELEAF CROSS

The Plough,
Lower Cadsden.

P

START/FINISH

the highest part along the fence! Ellesborough Warren below has the largest stand of box, a small evergreen tree and shrub, in Britain. It makes a refreshing break to leave the open grassland and drop into this silent, damp gorge wrapped in miniature spindle trees.

PULPIT HILL: The walk from Ellesborough Warren over Pulpit Hill and down to Lower Cadsden is all protected now and rich in grassland and woodland species. Over 50 different birds are known to breed in the area while the open slopes are rich in butterflies.

On Pulpit Hill itself is the most complete and accessible of all the Chiltern hillforts. It is square with a double bank, but quite small and it probably never had permanent settlement.

(Since I walked this area the National Trust have acquired the land so the ambiguous route around and down from Pulpit Hill may be improved in the years to come.)

LOWER CADSDEN: Small hamlet with a well hidden pub in the bottom of a valley surrounded on most sides by beech woods.

REFRESHMENTS:

THE RED LION, Upper Icknield Way, Whiteleaf. Pretty pub in old part of village with excellent food. Open 11 am to 3 pm and 6 pm to 11 pm. Telephone: 01844 344476.

THE BERNARD ARMS, Risborough Road, Great Kimble. Hotel and restaurant visited by Prime Ministers. Marks start of Midshires Way long distance path. Open 11 am to 3 pm (2.30 pm on Sundays) and 6 pm to 11 pm. Telephone: 01844 46173.

THE PLOUGH, Cadsden Road, Lower Cadsden. Secluded but still popular, mainly with ramblers. Open 12 noon to 2.30 pm and 5.30 pm to 11 pm. Telephone: 01844 343302.

Ellesborough

Walk 5
THE LEE
Length 5 miles

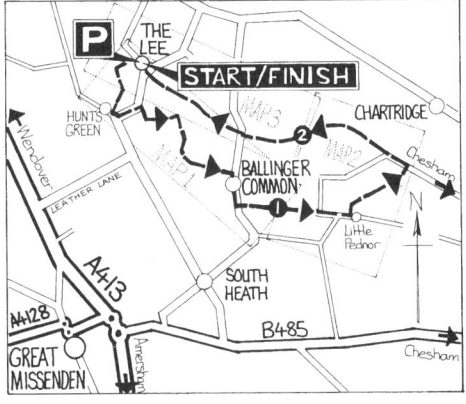

The Lee

GETTING THERE: Head north towards Aylesbury on the A413 from Amersham and go around Great Missenden on the bypass. Carry on over the two roundabouts and after about ½ mile there is a road called Leather Lane on your right, signposted to The Lee. Turn up here and then turn left at the T-junction on top of the hill. The road passes along an avenue of trees with a sharp right and then left turn before reaching the Cock and Rabbit pub. Turn left in front of it and park either around the green or slightly further on next to the church.

INTRODUCTION: This is a walk with a surprise on every turn, from the rustic old church hidden behind the new, to the aggressive glare of Admiral Howe's head appearing over a hedge; from Pednor House whose courtyard straddles the road to Chesham, to the tiny St Mary's church which appears in someone's front garden! In

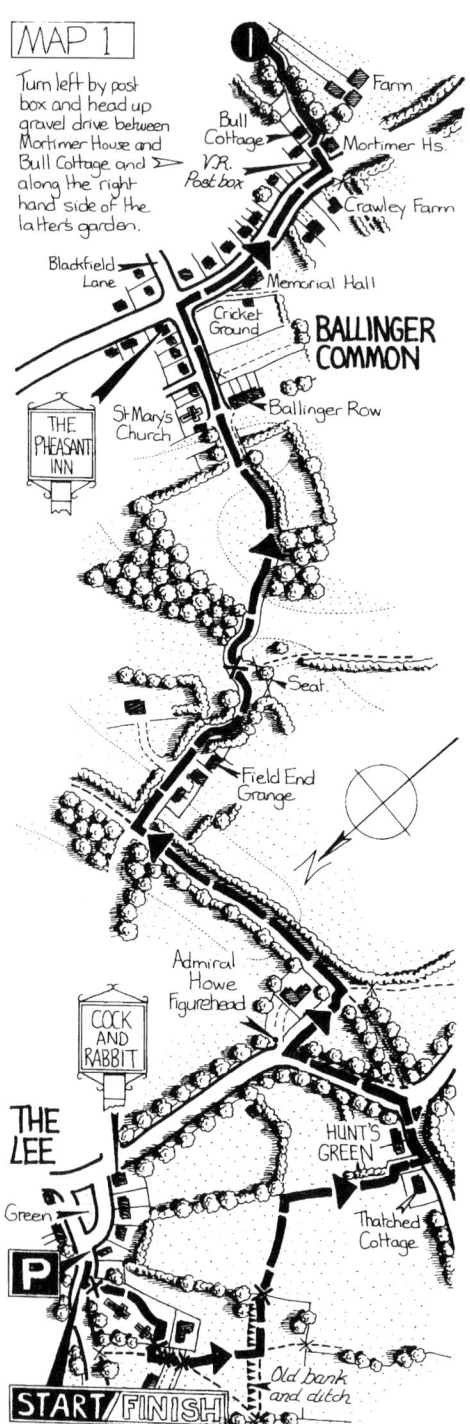

MAP 1

Turn left by post box and head up gravel drive between Mortimer House and Bull Cottage and ➤ along the right hand side of the latter's garden.

Farm

Bull Cottage

Mortimer Hs.

V.R. Post box

Crawley Farm

Blackfield Lane

Memorial Hall

Cricket Ground

BALLINGER COMMON

THE PHEASANT INN

St. Mary's Church

Ballinger Row

Seat

Field End Grange

Admiral Howe Figurehead

COCK AND RABBIT

THE LEE

Green

HUNT'S GREEN

Thatched Cottage

P

Old bank and ditch

START/FINISH

between, the gently rolling fields and woods of this Chiltern plateau add further variety and at Pednor give commanding views down the claw-shaped valleys to Chesham.

To start the walk, from the green head up to the church and pass through the front gate. Follow the path around the left of the brick building, through some shrubs and up to the old church behind. Go right around the rear of this and cross the stile in the corner, then turn left and go over the two stiles and into the field ahead. Cross this halfway until you reach a path running along a grassed over bank then turn left and follow this up to the stile, which you cross. Continue, using the maps.

THE LEE: The name comes from 'Leah' meaning a clearing which was probably cut out of the woods in the area around the old church (judging by the earthworks in the fields behind it). By the 19th century there would have been only a scattering of cottages over open common land but the Liberty family changed all that. Arthur Lasenby Liberty was the son of a Chesham draper who after acquiring Regent Street premises in 1875 travelled the world building up his business. He purchased the Lee manor and transformed the house. He created the green in 1901, built the Guildroom in 1903, and erected the Cock and Rabbit pub on its present site in 1907. He also built large semis for his estate workers which with the original cottages complete this idyllic scene. The village outlived the family who had to sell the estate in 1953 to meet death duties.

ST JOHN THE BAPTIST CHURCH: The red brick building nearest the road was built in 1868 and modified in 1911. This is of no great note until you look behind it and find

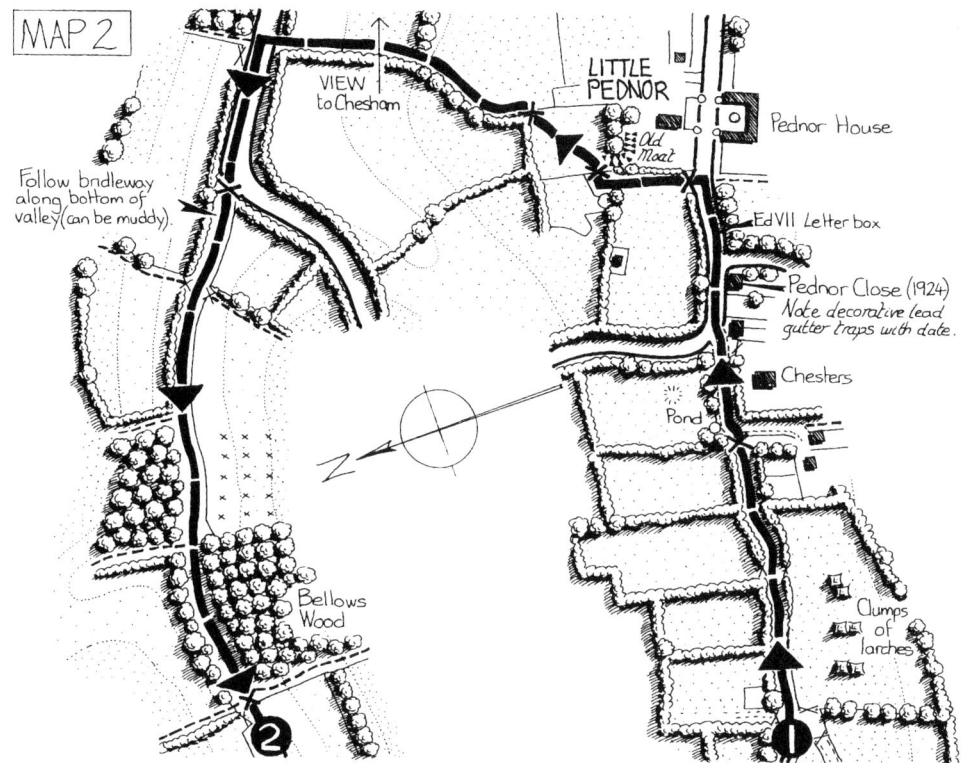

the original church has been retained. This humble and more attractive edifice dates in its earliest part to the 13th century while above the white rimmed south doorway you can just make out a scratched 'sundial' in the masonry.

ADMIRAL HOWE FIGUREHEAD: When rebuilding his shop in Regents Street into its present Mock Tudor frontage, Liberty purchased the last wooden ship built for the Navy. He used the wood for the frontage but the figurehead he sited on his estate at The Lee. This is of Admiral Howe who defeated the French on 'the Glorious First of June' in 1794.

BALLINGER COMMON: Until the 20th century an open tract of land with a string of cottages and farmhouses but now a tidy residential area where the original humble hovels are lost under later extensions. Of note is the tiny chapel which appears to be in a front garden yet proudly proclaims itself as St Mary's church.

PEDNOR HOUSE: A unique U-shaped building the courtyard of which is cut in two by the Chesham road. Although it is also known as Pednor Castle it only dates back to the turn of the 20th century, and was left deserted after a fire in 1933. The Royal Free in Hampstead renovated it in 1940 and used it as a maternity hospital to avoid the Blitz; 240 babies were delivered here up to March 1941!

Also of note is Pednor Close with its Arts and Crafts detailing, especially the

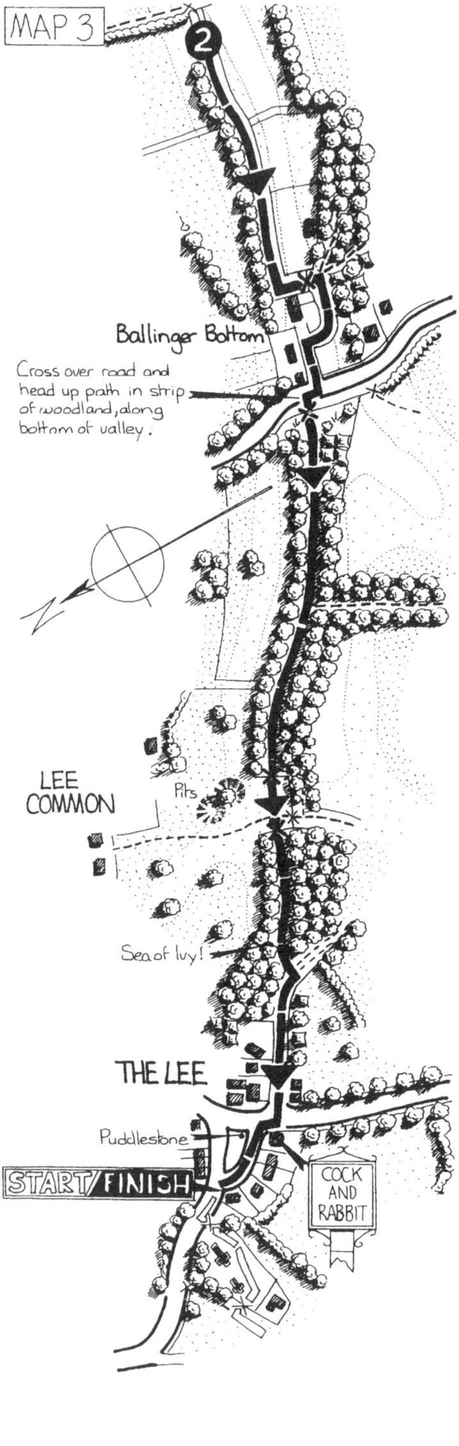

MAP 3

2

Ballinger Bottom

Cross over road and
head up path in strip
of woodland, along
bottom of valley.

LEE
COMMON

Pits

Sea of Ivy!

THE LEE

Puddlestone

START/FINISH

COCK
AND
RABBIT

elaborate guttering with its date pressed
into the lead.

BALLINGER BOTTOM: A row of old flint
and brick cottages which make a tidy
composition as you approach up the valley.
The walk from here to The Lee is along a
strip of woodland with a mix of beech and
conifers which has probably been influenced
by the estate.

PUDDLESTONE: See Walk 17.

REFRESHMENTS:
THE COCK AND RABBIT. Large pub with own beer
and good sized garden. Telephone: 01494 837540.
THE PHEASANT. Concentrates on food but still
has own beer. Telephone: 01494 837236.

The Lee

Walk 6
BLEDLOW
Length 4 miles

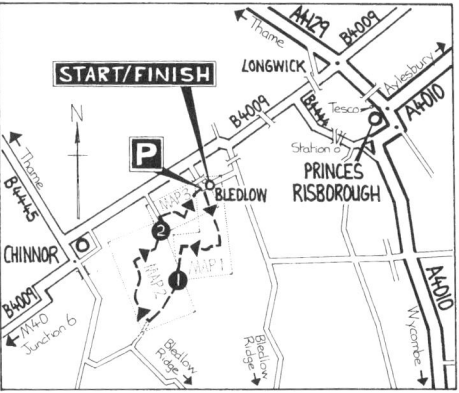

The Lions of Bledlow.

GETTING THERE: From the centre of Princes Risborough take the A4129 out of the town towards Thame. Just before Longwick turn left at the roundabout by the petrol station, and continue along the B4009 towards Chinnor. After passing under two railway bridges then a set of sharp bends the road straightens and there is a left-hand turn, West Lane, signposted to Bledlow (this is the third left after the roundabout). Head up this road, under another railway bridge and then find parking around the green or carry on to the left and park in the spaces by the telephone box.

INTRODUCTION: This walk passes through a truly ancient landscape with burial

mounds, a mysterious chalk cutting, and one of the oldest roads in the country. On the route you will pass through woods hanging above almost cliff-like slopes, admire views across the Vale below, and return beside the only preserved railway in the area. To finish with you can explore the tranquil and meandering village of Bledlow and its equally meandering pub!

BLEDLOW: The name Bledlow is Anglo-Saxon and probably means 'Bledda's Mound', although 'Bloody Hill' is a more colourful interpretation and refers to a supposed battle. The attractively set church is 13th-century but has among other work a more recent roof, judging by the higher pitched roof mark you can see on the east of the tower. This edifice stands above the Lyde, a deep gulley formed by a spring (see Hounslow Pond on Walk 14) which has now been landscaped for the award winning building that crowns its eastern edge. The remainder of the village includes the early 18th-century Manor House, a number of timber-framed cottages, and numerous trees which help maintain the rustic feel even where the 20th century has invaded.

THE COP TUMULUS: Although probably Bronze Age in origin, this burial mound has been used by the later Saxons to hold further bodies. One of

MAP 1

BLEDLOW

Telephone Box

START/FINISH

P

CAR PARK

THE LIONS OF BLEDLOW

N

PYLONS

Chalk Pit

Site of Inhumation and Chalk Pit

The Warren

Warren Cottage

Turn left at cottage and head up hill

HEMPTON WAINHILL

SIGN POST

Ridgeway Path

SIGN POST

Thickthorne Wood

Turn right, along Ridgeway until Hempton Wainhill

Bledlow Cross

Tumulus (The Cop)

Chalk Pit

Wain Hill

REFRESHMENTS:
THE LIONS OF BLEDLOW, Church End, Bledlow. Charismatic rambling pub with stone floor and timber beams (mind your head and feet!). Ample space to sit out the front on the green. Open 11 am to 3 pm and 6 pm to 11 pm; no food Sunday evening. Telephone: 01844 343345.

these had two broken limbs sometime in his life which they had tried to set, one of them successfully! A stone axe, 3,000 to 4,000 years old, was also found which had been brought up from Cornwall by our surprisingly well travelled ancestors.

A further Saxon inhumation was found in the chalk pit near the Warren and the bones found were reburied in the churchyard.

BLEDLOW CROSS: Although hidden by trees this little known cross is probably the oldest of all the local chalk cuttings. It is mentioned as 'Crouche' (French for cross) on charters dating from as early as 1260. To see it you will have to scramble up the bank on the track above Hempton Wainhill.

CHINNOR HILL: Virtually the whole area on Map 2 is part of this nature reserve. Of note are the juniper trees on the more exposed slopes but also look out for oak, ash, wild privet, spindle, buckthorn, hazel coppice and flowers including wild thyme, rockrose, candytuft and orchids.

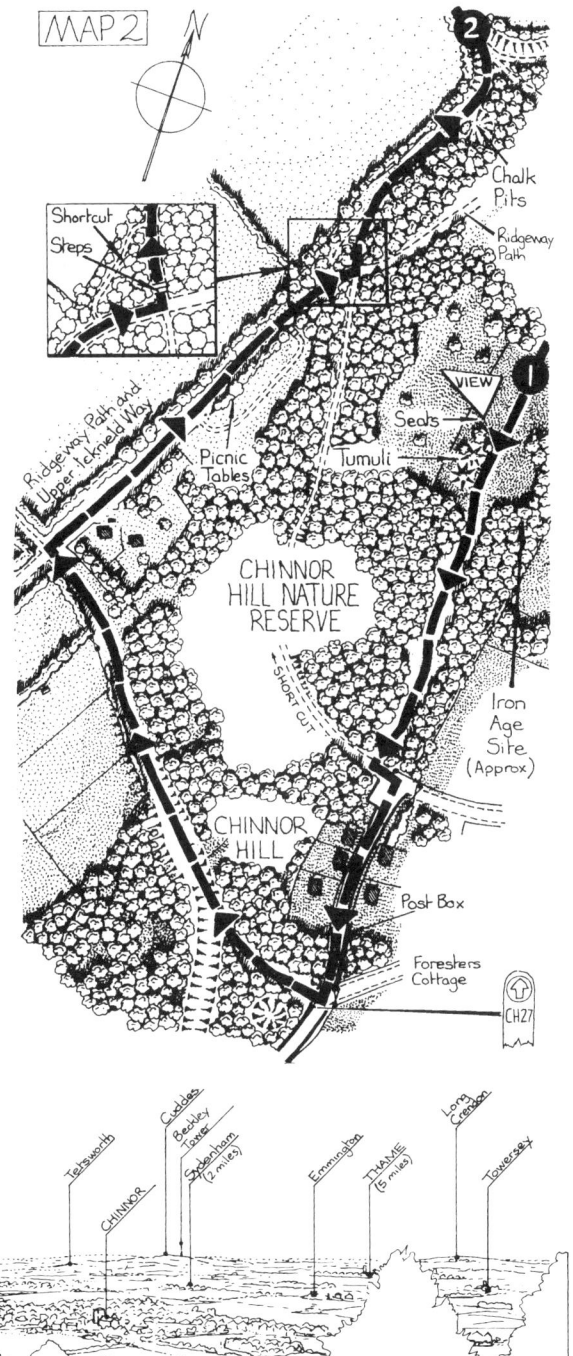

View from Point 1

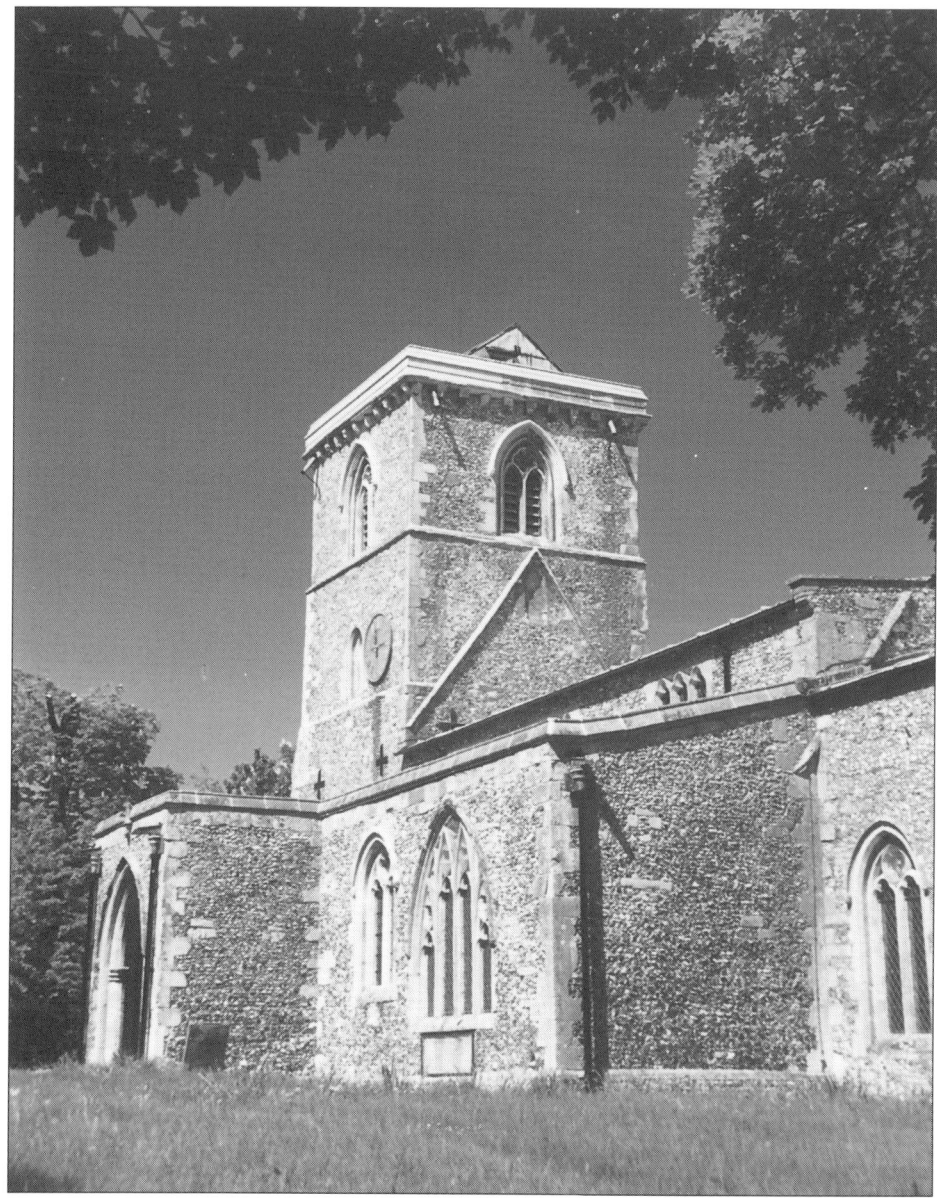

Bledlow church

TUMULI: These two burial mounds are under the clump of trees next to the viewpoint. They are probably Iron Age although Anglo-Saxon weapons were found. Nearby was a settlement of the same period where storage pits, pottery and iron pins have been uncovered. Unfortunately there is no clear sign under the encroaching scrub.

CHALK PITS: All along the walk you will notice old pits and quarries, some grassed over, some with exposed cliff faces of chalk and others lost under later tree cover. These were dug out from medieval times up to the 19th century to supply local farmers with the alkaline stone to sprinkle over their mainly acid fields in the Vale below. This helped balance the pH levels of the soil to increase crop yields.

ICKNIELD WAY: This was a major trading route used since Neolithic times. It would have taken the appearance of a wide strip of land, up to ½ mile in places, along which farmers herding livestock could have met traders from as far as Cornwall and Norfolk. Later the Romans built a road which is along the line of the present Lower Icknield Way. Today the Ridgeway Path runs along the track which is known as the Upper Icknield Way and as the name suggests it probably marks the top of this once wider route.

LOWER WAINHILL: This tiny hamlet has only a few cottages and a farm yet it still

justified a halt on the old Watlington Branch railway. This has been restored in traditional Great Western style and with its old level crossing creates a scene from a bygone age.

Numerous Roman remains have been found between here and Bledlow including a suspected villa in a clump of trees by the railway. Urns and skeletons have also been unearthed in Bledlow, among them a female body found in the side of the Lyde in 1928.

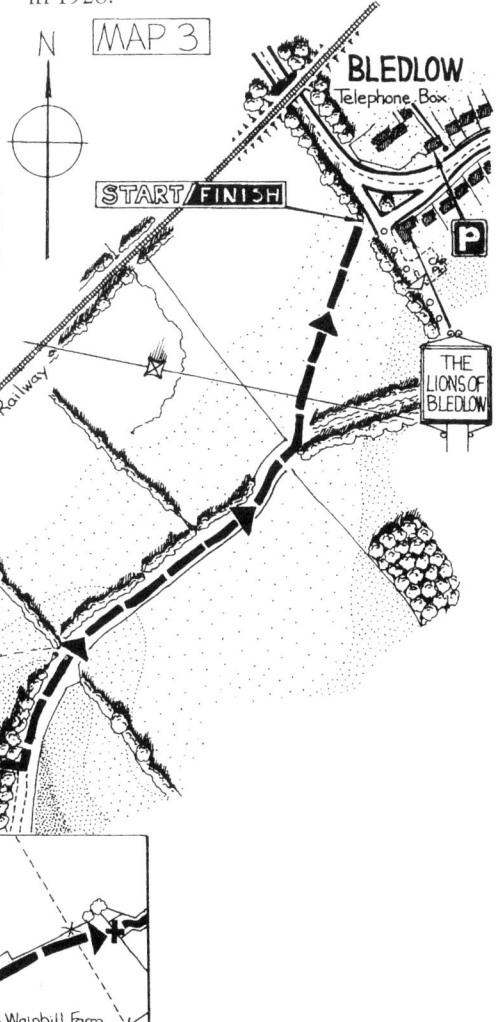

Walk 7
PARSLOWS HILLOCK
Length 3½ miles

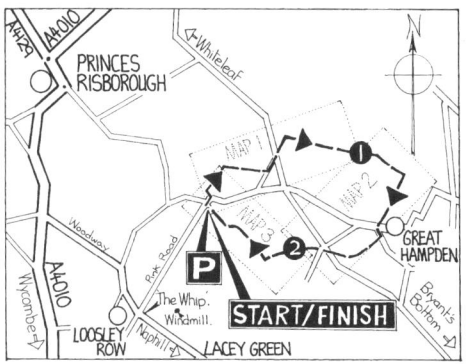

The Church of St Mary Magdalene

there is a crossroads after a small cutting; turn left here up Woodway and continue to Lacey Green. At the top of the steep hill turn left by the Whip pub and follow Pink Road for ½ mile until you reach Parslow's Hillock and the Pink and Lily pub. Park on the verge just before the pub.

INTRODUCTION:
   'Never came there to the Pink,
   Two such men as we I think,
   Never came there to the Lily,
   Two such men profoundly silly.'
So goes the short poem penned by Rupert Brook while visiting the area in 1913, before he went to war, found infamy and lost his life. The woods and hamlets on this high Chiltern plateau have changed little since

GETTING THERE: From Princes Risborough head south on the A4010 towards High Wycombe. Shortly after leaving the town

his day and Hampden House is still set among fields and parkland. Not only will you find yourself walking through this tranquil setting but also along the mysterious Grim's Ditch and the little known Black Hedge.

THE BLACK HEDGE: If you look at a map of the Chiltern escarpment you will notice that parish boundaries form strips which enclose a village at the foot of the hills and land up the slope and on top. These can date as far back as the Saxon period and recorded the rights of the manors in the Vale to the wood and grazing land above. Records still exist of one such boundary laid out in AD 903 around Monks Risborough; this is the Black Hedge. The name comes from the blackthorn trees from which it was composed. There are some lengths still visible today identifiable by a bank at the base of the hedge and a wide mix of trees and shrubs. Look out for ones with horizontal branches at their base which then suddenly turn upwards. These are trees used in traditional hedge laying which as the practice has died out have been left to grow vertically.

GRIM'S DITCH: These linear features which are found in numerous locations but mainly in the South are still of uncertain origin. Although they share the same name they are probably not related but were local boundaries to mark territory or keep livestock. As two tumuli have been raised on part of the bank near Hampden it is assumed that this length may date back more than 2,000 years while in other areas the ditches may be Saxon. It is worth noting that as they are straight it is likely there were no trees when they were dug. These would have blocked the line of sight when laying them out and falling trees would have dam-

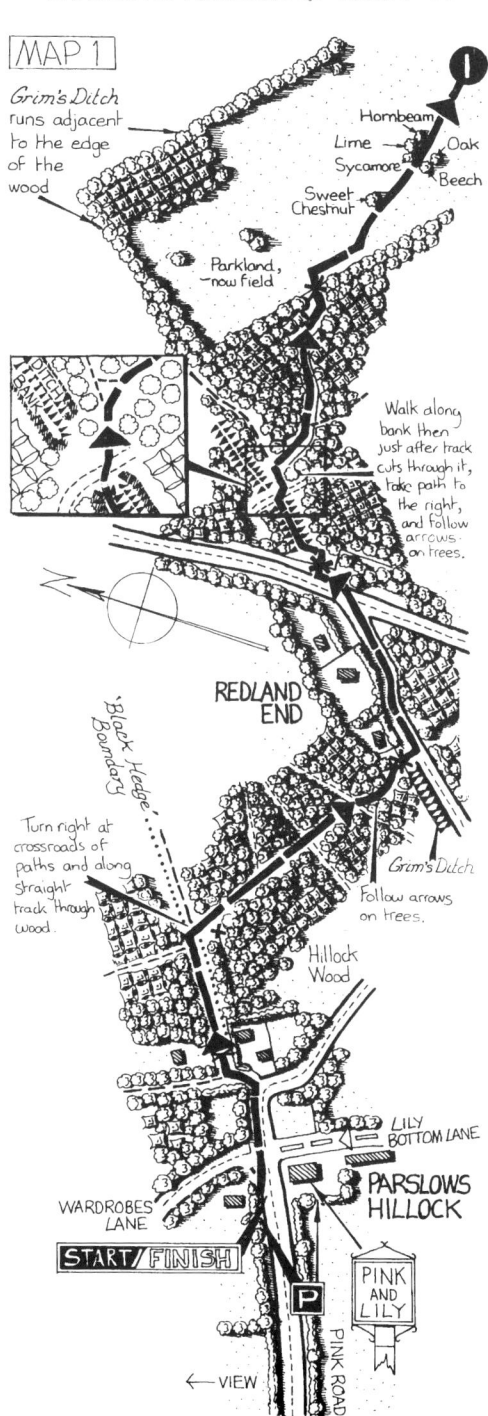

MAP 1

Grim's Ditch runs adjacent to the edge of the wood

Hornbeam
Lime
Sycamore
Oak
Beech
Sweet Chestnut

Parkland, now field

Walk along bank then just after track cuts through it, take path to the right, and follow arrows on trees.

REDLAND END

'Black Hedge' Boundary

Turn right at crossroads of paths and along straight track through wood.

Grim's Ditch
Follow arrows on trees.

Hillock Wood

LILY BOTTOM LANE

PARSLOWS HILLOCK

WARDROBES LANE

START/FINISH

P

PINK AND LILY

PINK ROAD

← VIEW

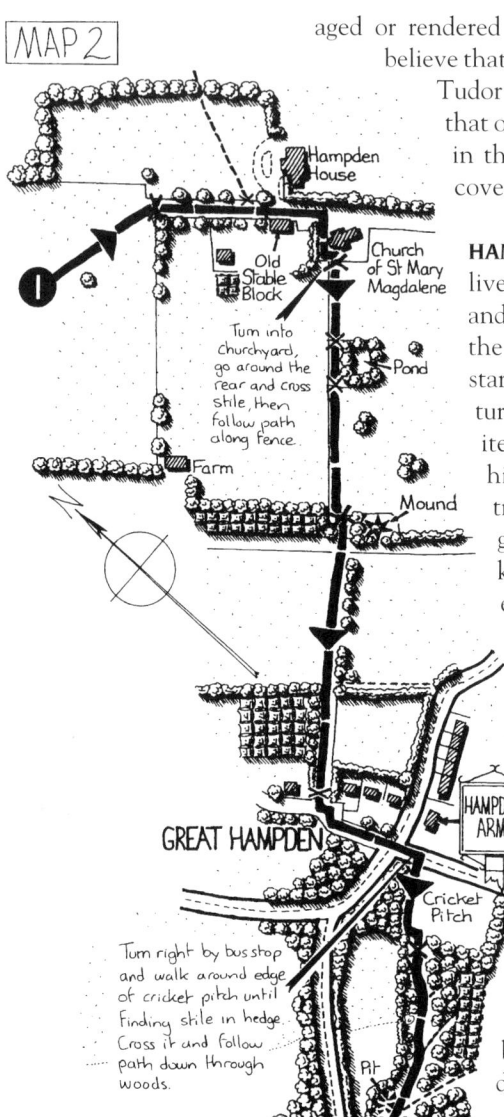

MAP 2

Hampden House

Old Stable Block

Turn into churchyard, go around the rear and cross stile, then follow path along fence.

Farm

Church of St Mary Magdalene

Pond

Mound

GREAT HAMPDEN

HAMPDEN ARMS

Cricket Pitch

Turn right by bus stop and walk around edge of cricket pitch until finding stile in hedge. Cross it and follow path down through woods.

Pit

Monkton Wood

Path can be vague due to tree felling; look out for arrows on trees.

aged or rendered the ditch useless. We often mistakenly believe that the country was a blanket of forest up until Tudor times. Modern archaeology has shown that our landscape fluctuates and there are times in the past when there has been as little tree cover as today.

HAMPDEN HOUSE: The Hampden family lived on this site before the Norman Conquest and there is still a doorway which dates from the medieval house. The present building was started by Griffith Hampden in the 16th century. It is said that when Queen Elizabeth visited, she was disappointed by the view from his new home. So Griffith had an avenue of trees cut down while she slept to give her a glorious vista the next morning. This is still known as the Queen's Avenue. The gothic exterior was added in the 18th century shortly before the house passed to a new family only to become a school and now a management centre.

JOHN HAMPDEN, 'The Patriot': Buckinghamshire's most famous son, born in 1594, was a cousin of Oliver Cromwell and Member of Parliament for Grampound. In 1626 he made his famous stand against the Ship Money which King Charles had demanded to finance another attack on France. His opposition landed him in jail for two years but by the time he was free the King had dissolved Parliament. When the monarch demanded further Ship Money in 1635 Hampden's resistance to pay gave other counties the will to withhold payment. This shortfall in his finances forced Charles to recall Parliament in 1640. One act which further ignited the already tense situation was when a group of apprentices (known as Roundheads due to their cropped haircuts) were attacked by out of work soldiers who referred to themselves as Cavaliers. These names were used by the opposing sides in the ensuing Civil War. Hampden was killed early in the campaign after being shot at Chalgrove Fields, but his son Richard went on to serve Cromwell and became Chancellor of the Exchequer. It was Richard who sold the family's London residence to a George Downing who then built a row of houses on the land and named the street after himself. No 10 in this street is now quite famous!

PINK AND LILY: The odd name of this pub is a bit of a mystery. The local story is that a Mr Pink and a Mrs Lily worked at Hampden House in the early 1800s and the pub was so named after they married. On the other hand it stands on the corner of Lily Bottom Lane and Pink Hill so this source may be more realistic if less romantic! When Rupert Brooke visited here earlier this century it was a solid, square building with massive chimneys which was already over a hundred years old. Today it has expanded inside and out and offers a wider range of beers and food than Brooke could ever have imagined, but the old bar at the front which bears his name has been retained.

> **REFRESHMENTS:**
> THE PINK AND LILY is open from 11.45 am to 3 pm and 6 pm to 11 pm; no food Sunday evening. Telephone: 01494 488308.

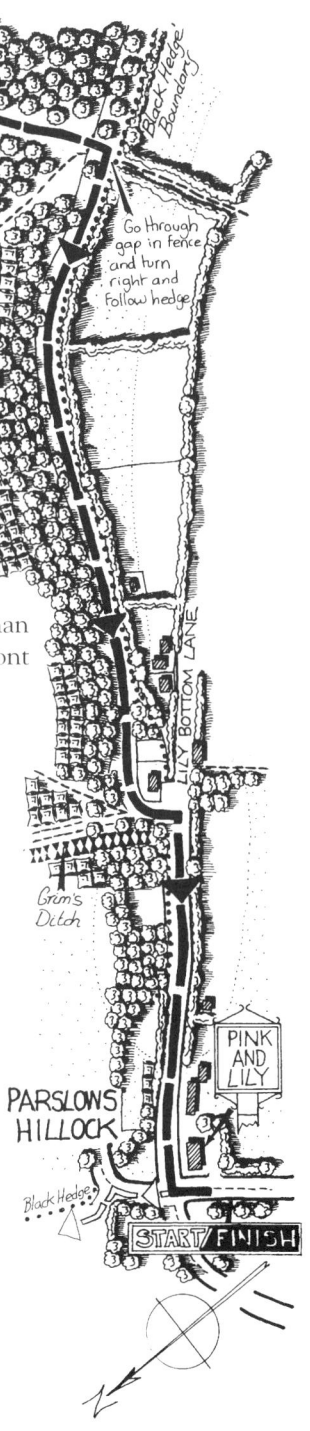

Walk 8
LITTLE MISSENDEN
Length 4½ miles

The Manor House

GETTING THERE: Little Missenden is just off the A413 between Amersham and Great Missenden. Follow the signs off the main road depending on which direction you are coming and follow what is the old A road into the village centre. Parking is easiest in the southern end of the village on the opposite side of the road from the Red Lion.

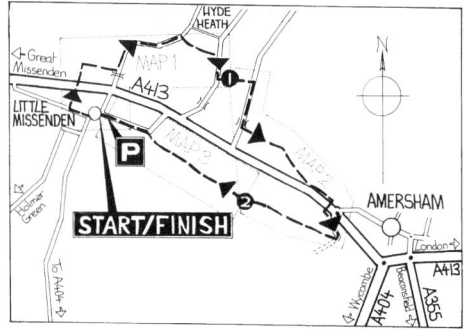

INTRODUCTION: I had barely started this walk myself when I was halted by a frantic Frenchman armed with a walkie talkie. Oh no, the curse of every Chiltern village, the dreaded 'Period Drama Film Crew'! You can hardly blame them, the imposing brick manor house, the rusticated church and rows of undulating cottages make for an ideal backdrop to yet another sentimental detective story. There is more to the area though than this chocolate box image. The walk takes you past the site of a motte and bailey castle, through mixed woodland with ancient boundaries, and back along the

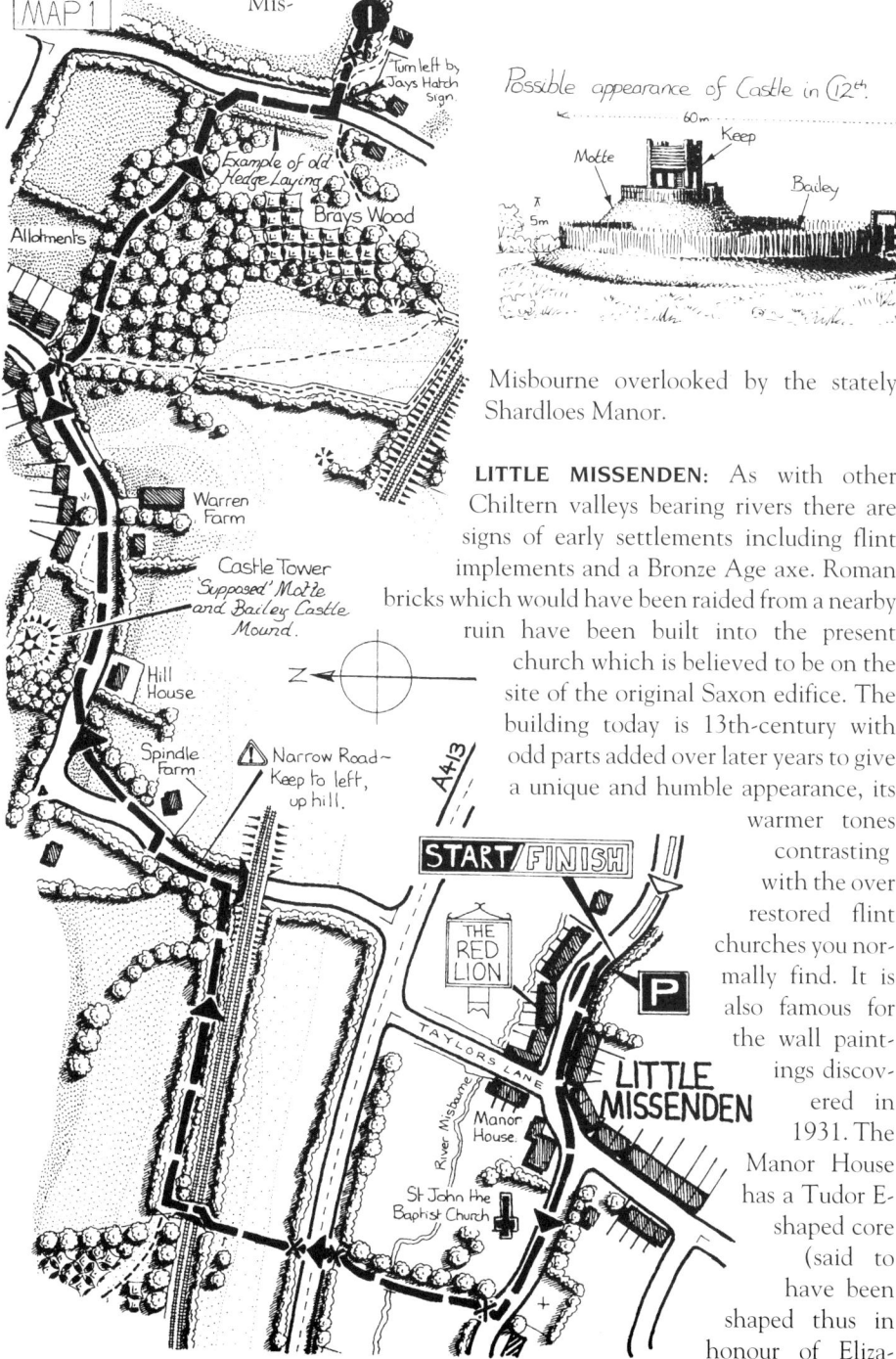

MAP 1

Mis-

Turn left by Jays Hatch Sign.

Example of old Hedge Laying

Brays Wood

Allotments

Possible appearance of Castle in 12th.

← 60m →

Motte

Keep

Bailey

5m

Warren Farm

Castle Tower 'Supposed' Motte and Bailey Castle Mound.

Hill House

Spindle Farm

Narrow Road~ Keep to left, up hill.

A413

N ←

START/FINISH

THE RED LION

P

TAYLORS LANE

River Misbourne

Manor House.

St John the Baptist Church

LITTLE MISSENDEN

Misbourne overlooked by the stately Shardloes Manor.

LITTLE MISSENDEN: As with other Chiltern valleys bearing rivers there are signs of early settlements including flint implements and a Bronze Age axe. Roman bricks which would have been raided from a nearby ruin have been built into the present church which is believed to be on the site of the original Saxon edifice. The building today is 13th-century with odd parts added over later years to give a unique and humble appearance, its warmer tones contrasting with the over restored flint churches you normally find. It is also famous for the wall paintings discovered in 1931. The Manor House has a Tudor E-shaped core (said to have been shaped thus in honour of Elizabeth I) with a massive brick frontage of the 18th century. The pineapples each side of the doorway were popular in the 17th century as a 'welcome' sign.

CASTLE TOWER: This motte and bailey castle was probably linked to the manor held by Thomas Mantle in 1086 (now Mantles Farm). In the civil unrest of King Stephen's reign (1135-1154) local barons erected their own castles in defiance of the Crown, and this could have been one of these. Such buildings would usually only have stood for a short time and it is lucky that 800 years on this mound and ditch are still, if only just, visible.

SHARDLOES: The house that was purchased by the Drake family in 1632 was higher up the hill than the later mansion you can see today. The Drakes were influential in the area and the almshouses they financed still stand in Amersham High Street. Shardloes was built in the mid 18th century and this included the widening of the lake and the resiting of the road north, to its present route. Its old route is now the path the walk returns along and gives an excellent view of this grand house.

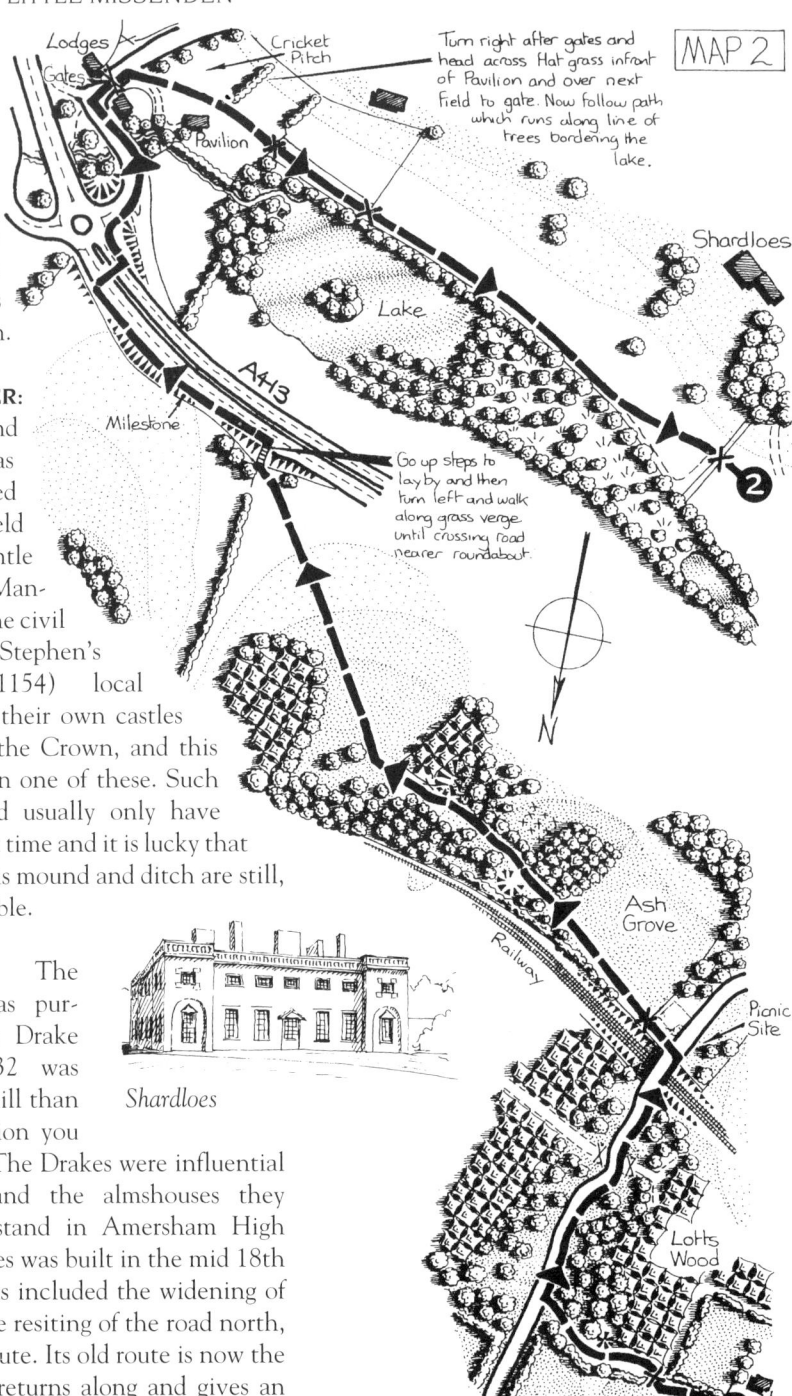

Shardloes

MAP 2

Turn right after gates and head across flat grass in front of Pavilion and over next field to gate. Now follow path which runs along line of trees bordering the lake.

Go up steps to layby and then turn left and walk along grass verge until crossing road nearer roundabout.

Lodges
Gates
Cricket Pitch
Pavilion
Shardloes
Lake
A413
Milestone
Ash Grove
Railway
Picnic Site
Lotts Wood
N

RIVER MISBOURNE: This notoriously unreliable stream has been running dry for centuries. Despite this it had sufficient depth for a 35 lb pike which was caught in 1879 and for otters which lived around Shardloes up until the 1940s. Abstraction from London has been blamed in recent years for its almost permanent lack of water but evaporation accounts for three times as much! The river is best viewed from the rear of the Red Lion where in wetter years trout can be seen.

St John's, Little Missenden.

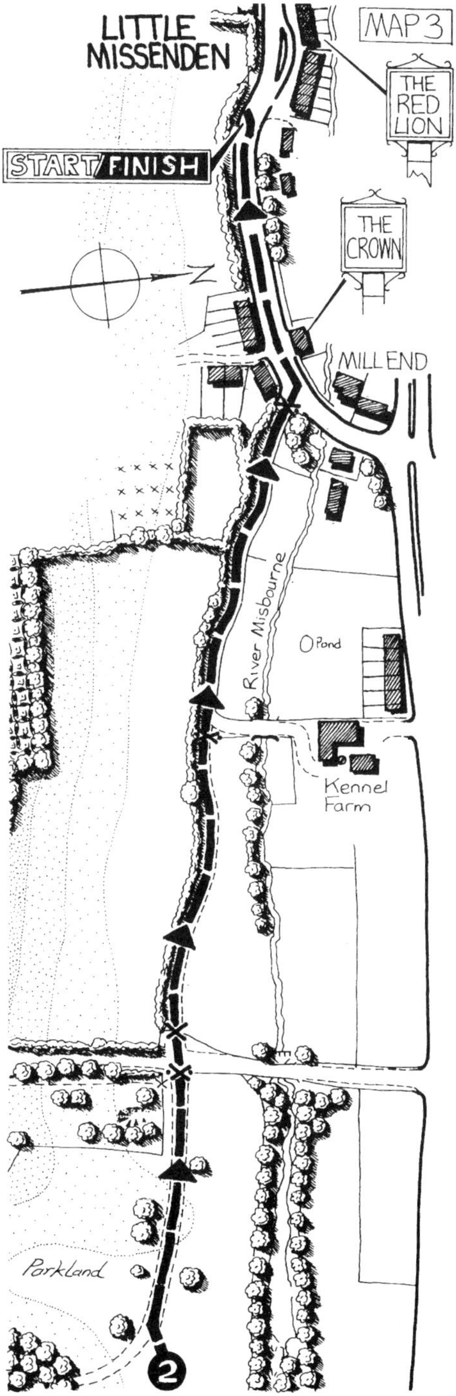

REFRESHMENTS:

THE RED LION, Little Missenden. Rustic local with 350 year old fireplace and river running through garden. Open 11 am to 2.30 pm and 5.30 pm to 11 pm. Telephone: 01494 862876.

THE CROWN, Mill End. Welcoming, genuine village pub. Open 11 am to 2.30 pm and 6 pm to 11 pm. Telephone: 01494 862571.

Walk 9
RADNAGE
Length 4½ miles

St Mary's church

GETTING THERE: From the centre of High Wycombe take the A40 out of town and through West Wycombe. At the end of the village turn right up Chorley Road, signposted to Bledlow Ridge. At the end of the long straight and just before the road heads uphill, turn left and continue past the farm. Ignore the next left turn and carry on the suddenly narrowing road as it meanders for the next few miles. Eventually you come upon some houses on the left and then a T-junction by a pond. Go right and keep on this road as it twists and turns until after ½ mile a driveway appears on the right, leading to the church. This is the easiest place to park but please be careful not to restrict access.

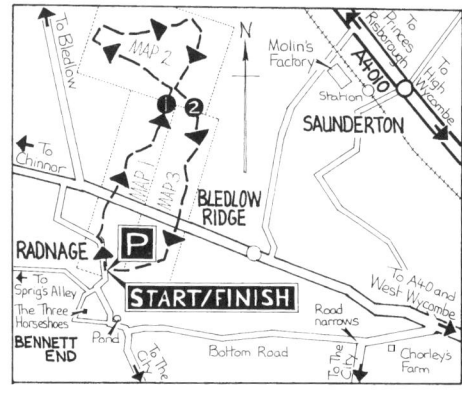

INTRODUCTION: It comes as a pleasant surprise that only a few miles from the hustle and bustle of Wycombe is a valley which seems cut off from the modern world. In a time when busy roads break up the countryside and the sprawl of suburbia swallows up the remains it is reassuring to know there are secret havens like Radnage.

This is a walk of rounded hollows, grassy ridges and tree tunnels. The route goes from one remote valley to another, commanding spectacular views with a climb over the odd, pebble-shaped Lodge Hill.

RADNAGE: With its earliest spellings being Radenach, Radenai and Radenhach and with the manor having been in the hands of Fontenault Abbey this tiny English hamlet seems to have had surprising French connections. St Mary's is of an unusual construction: notice that the central tower is narrower than the nave and chancel it is sandwiched between. This has similarities with churches in Brittany, reinforcing its foreign heritage. The main body of the church is 12th-century with internal furnishings which include wall paintings and a pre-Norman font uncovered in a neighbouring field!

People were living in the area long before this. Just up the road in Sprig's Alley in 1923, workmen repairing a carriageway found a Roman glass bowl and an amber jug. These are still of sufficient note to be on permanent display in the British Museum.

ROUTS GREEN: The earliest settlement along Bledlow Ridge was probably in this area with a chapel mentioned in 1341. The lack of water limited development along the Ridge until the 20th century despite the digging of a deep well at Moorlands Farm which was said to have reached 600 ft before it collapsed. Drinking water was

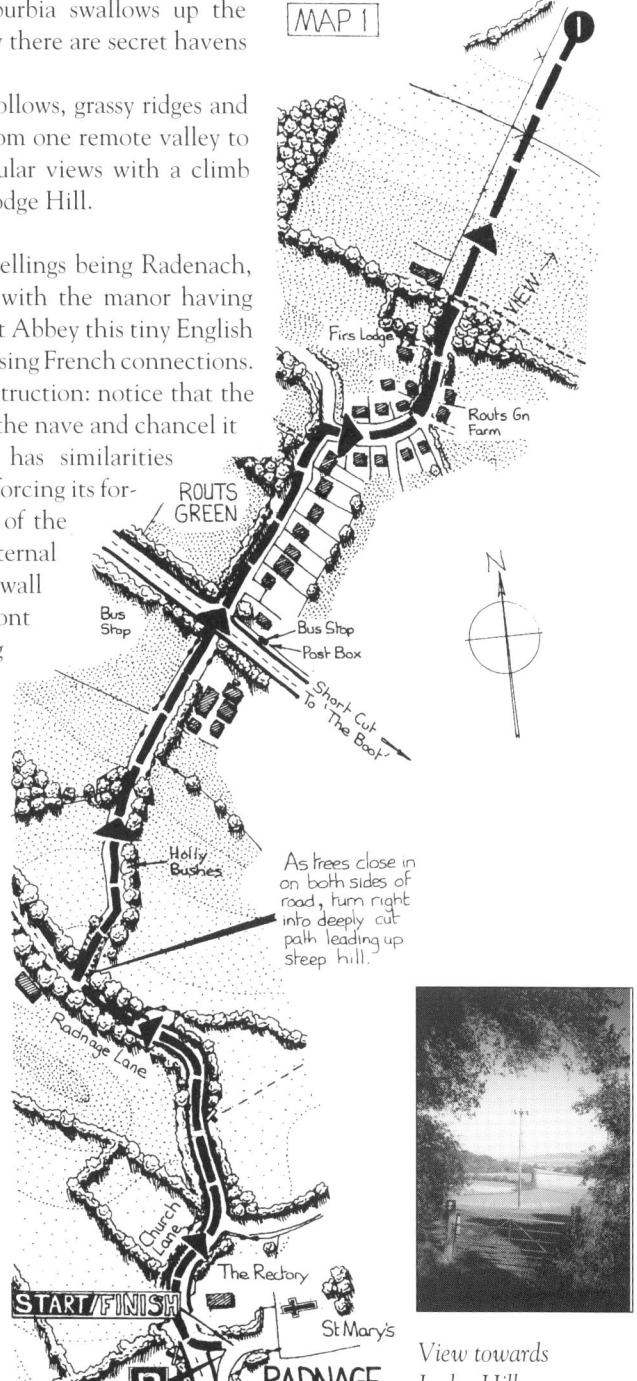

As trees close in on both sides of road, turn right into deeply cut path leading up steep hill.

View towards Lodge Hill.

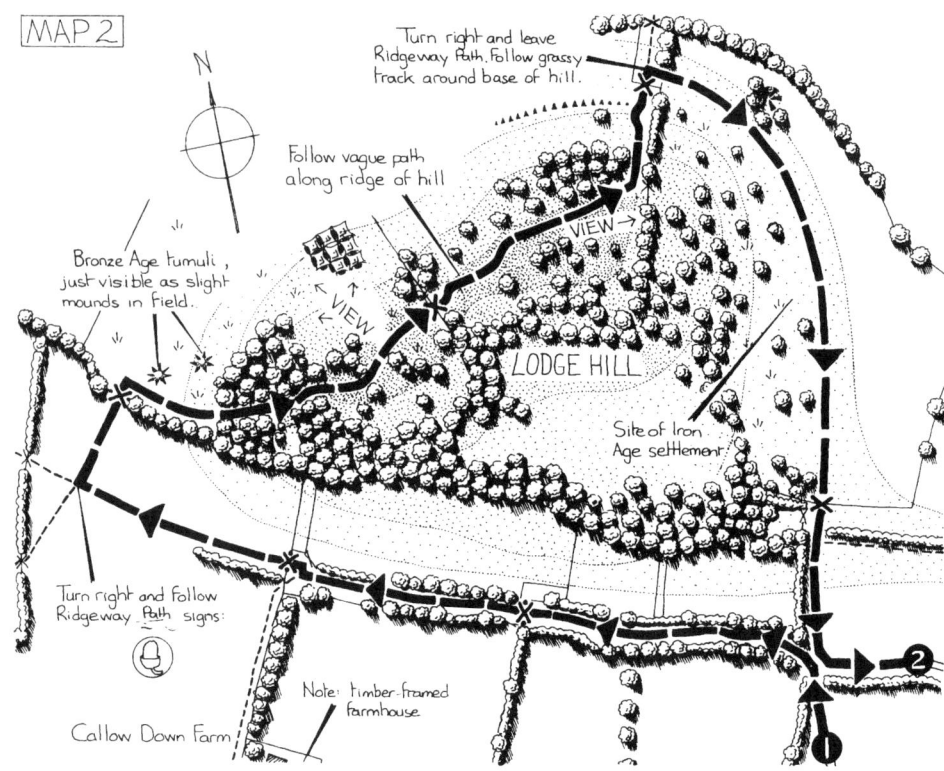

MAP 2

Turn right and leave Ridgeway Path. Follow grassy track around base of hill.

Follow vague path along ridge of hill

Bronze Age tumuli, just visible as slight mounds in field.

VIEW →

← VIEW

LODGE HILL

Site of Iron Age settlement

Turn right and follow Ridgeway Path signs.

Note: timber-framed farmhouse

Callow Down Farm

often collected off roofs, that from a tin one being preferable to water off a thatch! There were numerous ponds along the tracks for cattle, a few of which survive though most traces of the past are under housing which today lines the roads.

LODGE HILL: This prominent sand-capped mound appears to rise out of the valley bottom in its own right although it is at one end of a low ridge which runs down to West Wycombe. This ridge has attracted people long before us. There are a number of tumuli, Bronze Age burial mounds, which date from 1500-2500 BC. Two of these are visible at the west end of the hill. Such tumuli were constructed by raising a

wooden chamber usually over a single inhumation and then covering it with a mound of earth. Unfortunately if the plough has not destroyed them then Victorian treasure hunters have more than likely removed their contents.

On the eastern side of the hill was an Iron Age settlement where a ditch surrounded circular huts more than 2,000 years ago. To

REFRESHMENTS:

THE THREE HORSESHOES, Bennett End. Rustic 200 year old pub hidden up a back lane south of the church (see area map). Open 12 noon to 2.30 pm and 7 pm to 11 pm. Telephone: 01494 483273.

the west of the aforementioned barrows a further site has also been discovered. Add to this a number of other finds, including Roman villas, cremation urns, coins and flint tools, and it's clear to see this was a popular location in prehistory. This trend thankfully has not continued today and leaves Lodge Hill rich in a mixed range of flora. This diversity, particularly on top where it is effected by the sandy soil, can be appreciated by all, that is if you are not too busy admiring the views!

MURDER IN YOESDEN WOOD: When John Kingham heard shots on an autumn day in 1893 he suspected poachers and marched off into the woods to confront them. When he did not return a search was started and the next day his body was found. John Avery, who was in the area at the time and had heard gunshots and voices, was an important witness but things took a turn for the worse when bloodstained clothes and a knife were found in his house. Despite identifying the voice he heard with Kingham as that of Jim Brooks, he was arrested and went to court. Unfortunately his brother, Richard Avery, was also held when a shirt covered in blood was discovered; things looked grim for them both! But during the proceedings witnesses confirmed that neither could have been in the woods at the time and on closer inspection the knife discovered was too blunt to inflict the wounds found on Kingham. The case collapsed when witnesses confirmed that only one person had threatened Kingham and that this same person had also threatened Richard Avery. This was the brother of Jim Brooks who had been heard in the woods prior to the murder, but no one was ever convicted. Richard Avery always claimed he knew the murderer but he took the name with him to his grave.

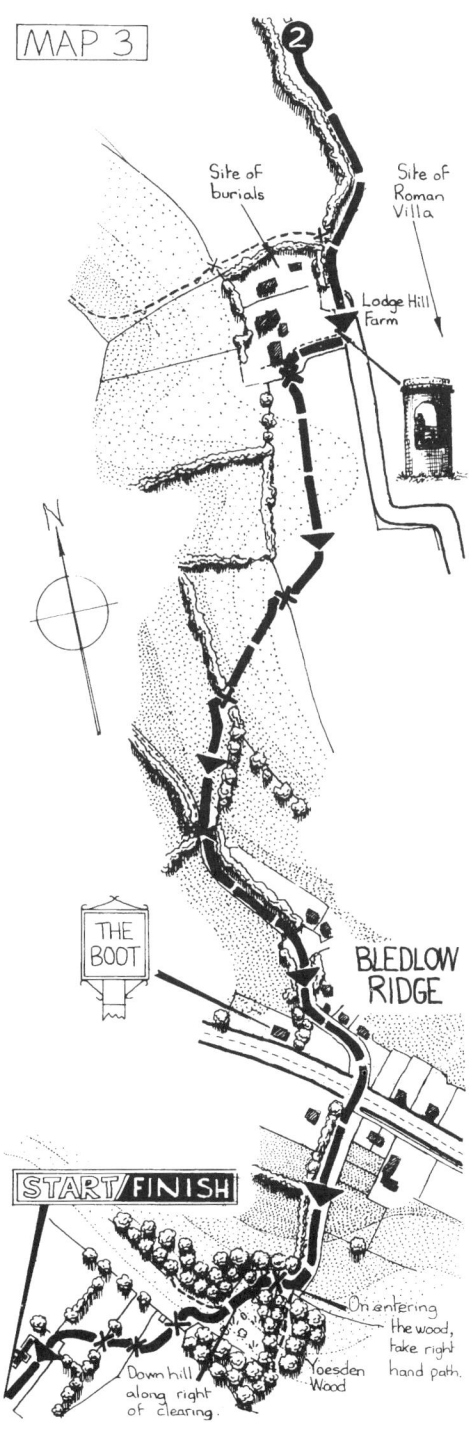

Walk 10
CHENIES
Length 4½ miles

Dodds Mill

GETTING THERE: Chenies is just off the A404 between Amersham and Rickmansworth. From junction 18 on the M25 take the A404 towards Amersham and head through Chorleywood, past a large school on the left and out into the country. After about ½ mile turn right down the road signposted to Chenies. You will shortly see on your right the Red Lion pub and the best place to park is along the roadside opposite. There are parking spaces further on in the village but these tend to be limited.

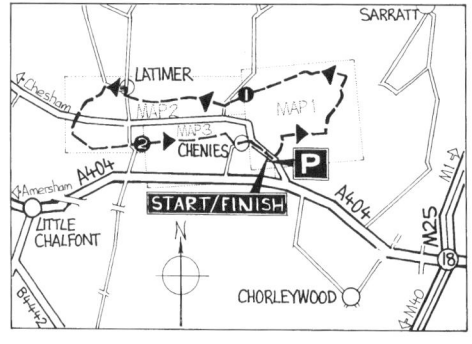

INTRODUCTION: A memorable walk thanks to the 'well watered' river Chess and the dramatic views over it from the adjacent hills. This fertile valley has remained remarkably remote from the surrounding suburban sprawl and is bypassed by the main arterial roads, preserving its pastures and meadows. The route takes you past the sites of two Roman villas, two Tudor mansions (one genuine, one fake), two model villages with two triangular greens, and two oddities – the Liberty Tomb and a young oak planted in the stump of its predecessor.

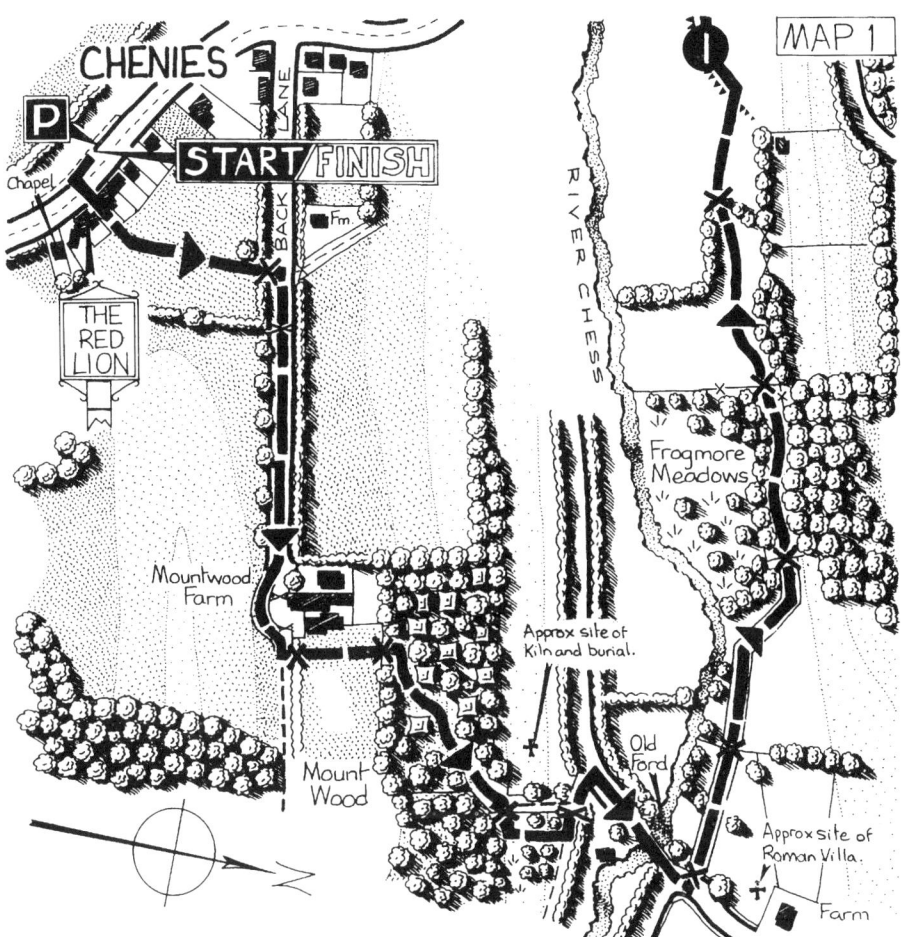

CHAPEL: Symmetrical, simple and stark in contrast to the alternative place of worship at St Michael's. This honest edifice dates from 1778 but had already been refaced by 1800.

ROMAN SITES: Discovered more recently than the Latimer villa is a building at Valley Farm, and a working area with a kiln on the other side of the river. An infant burial was found at the latter site (see Walk 20) and there have also been occasional finds along the road up to the ford which must have been a crossing of some antiquity.

DODDS MILL: The mill has served Chenies since the 12th century. It was owned by the Dodds family in the 1700s and under them it was converted to a paper mill. The building probably dates from this period as it lapsed in use by the mid 19th century.

LATIMER: This was originally known as Isenhampstead, but the Latimer family, who owned the manor from 1331, added their name to it, until the 19th century when the former part was dropped. The Latimers' house had been on the site since the 13th century but when Charles I was taken here in the years before his execution it was in the hands of the Cavendish family. It was they who cleared most of the village in the 1750s to enlarge their grounds! The present house was built in the 1830s in an Elizabethan style and St Mary's church followed in 1841 to replace the old medieval chapel. Today the village is a tidy mix of older timber-framed structures and Victorian estate buildings around a picturesque green complete with a 19th-century pump.

ROMAN VILLA (site of): In 1834, while building the main Chesham road, workmen uncovered a Roman flooring and four skeletons. Later excavations revealed a U-shaped villa with a courtyard dating from AD 180 which was abandoned towards the end of the 4th century.

CHENIES: As with Latimer it was the family who owned the manor, in this case the Cheynes, who added their name to Isenhampstead until it became just Chenies in the last century. In 1526 their house passed on to the Russells or, as they became known after 1550, the Earls of Bedford. They rebuilt the manor house, adding the main south wing to the earlier west, and it is these two parts which make up the building you see today (courtesy of some remodelling in 1830).

The ruined 'tower' as you first approach the house is probably part of the original building as is the undercroft near the church. The house is also surrounded by

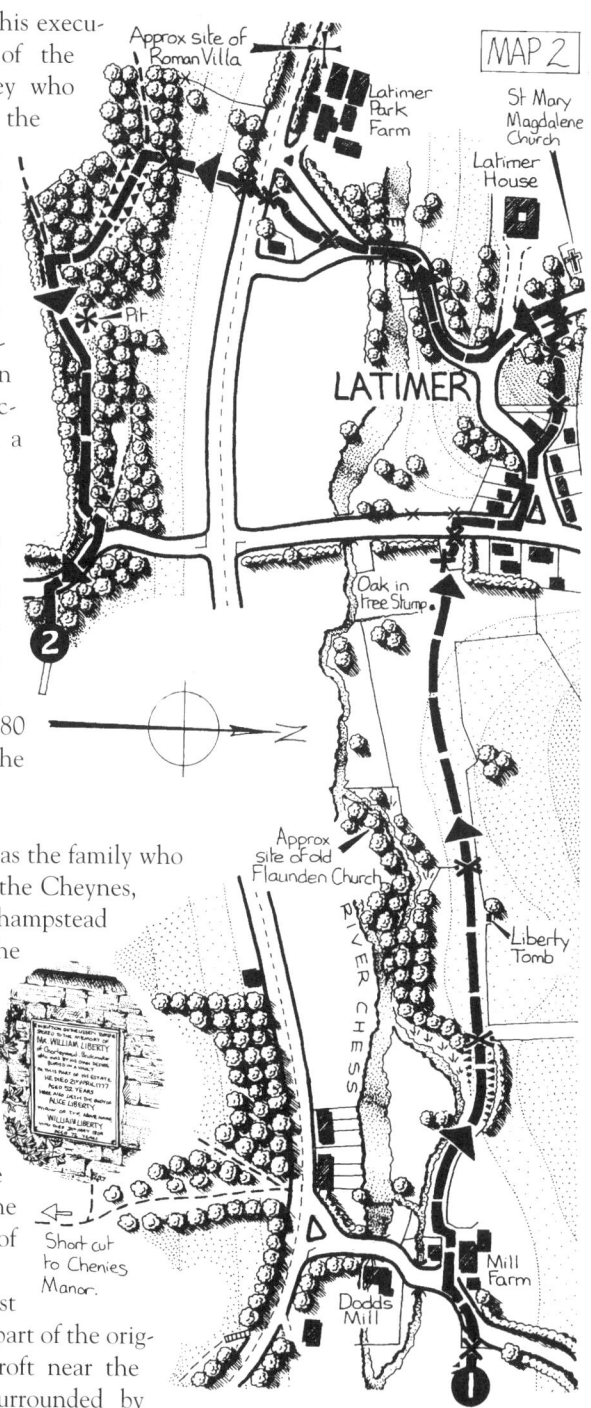

MAP 3

START/FINISH

THE RED LION

THE BEDFORD ARMS

CHENIES

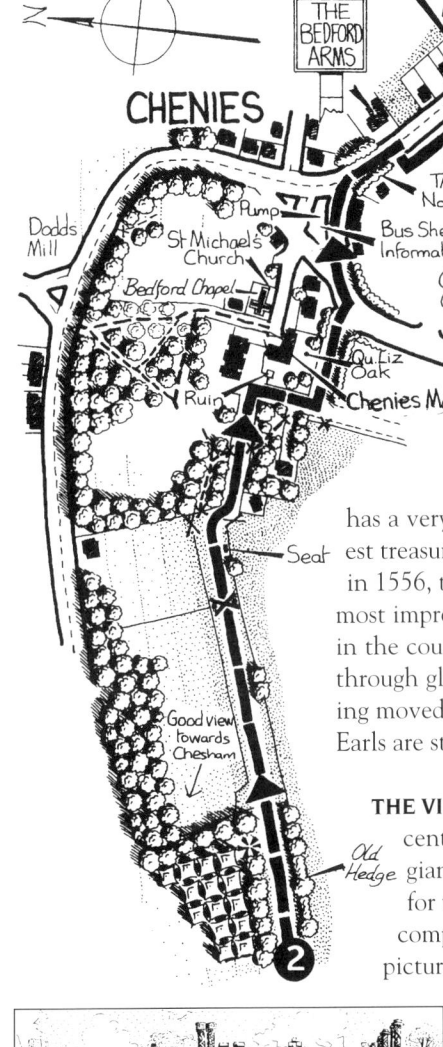

TAKE CARE - No Pavement

Pump

Dodds Mill

St Michael's Church

Bedford Chapel

Bus Shelter with Information board.

Chenies Garden Centre

Quiz Oak

Ruin

Chenies Manor

Seat

Good view towards Chesham

Old Hedge

2

The old ford near Chenies.

notable gardens making it worth a visit in its own right. It is open from April to October, on Wednesdays and Thursdays only, between 2 pm and 5 pm.

ST MICHAEL'S CHURCH: The church is over 500 years old and has a very unified Perpendicular air about it. The greatest treasure though is the chapel, affixed to its north side in 1556, to house the deceased Earls of Bedford. It is the most impressive collection of tombs of any parish church in the country; unfortunately you can only peek at them through glass doors from inside the church. Despite having moved the family home to Woburn centuries ago the Earls are still laid to rest here.

THE VILLAGE: The majority of the buildings are 19th-century estate houses interspersed with some Georgian and earlier timber-framed cottages. Look out for their dates in the brickwork. The green with its compulsory Victorian pump completes the idyllic picture.

CHENIES MANOR

REFRESHMENTS:
THE RED LION, Chenies. Friendly free house devoid of modern machines, with notable snug bar. Open 11 am to 2.30 pm and 5.30 pm to 11 pm. Telephone: 01923 282722.
THE BEDFORD ARMS, Chenies. Upmarket establishment, but has two bars and still has bar food. Open 11 am to 3.30 pm and 5.30 pm to 11 pm. Telephone: 01923 283301.

Walk 11
LEWKNOR
Length 3½ miles

View from Aston Hill.

GETTING THERE: Leave the M40 at junction 6, the B4009 Princes Risborough to Watlington road, and turn toward the latter town. After a few hundred yards turn right down Watlington Road and into Lewknor village.

To park, use the roadside as near to the Olde Leathern Bottel pub as space will allow.

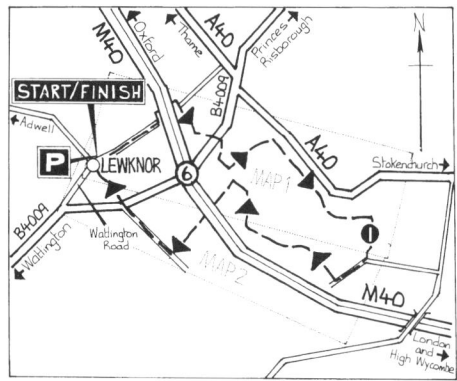

INTRODUCTION: Dramatic views and wildlife bless this walk of contrasts – from the surprisingly tranquil streets of Lewknor with its stone church standing above the springs which burst out of the scarp here, to the climb through the mighty, high beech woods of Aston Hill. Then return down open grassland and scrub while birds of prey and deer pass tantalisingly close.

LEWKNOR: There has been continuous settlement in this area since at least the Iron Age, but the 'or' ending to the name indicates that its predecessor was further up the escarpment. St Margaret's church has late Norman origins but more noticeable is the fact that the roof on the east end is higher than the main body of the building. The middle would have been higher but was later rebuilt with a flatter pitch as was the style in the 15th century, but the money didn't stretch to the chancel!

Behind the church under a misleading shell of breeze block and corrugated iron is an ancient timber frame now used as a barn. It was only discovered in 1969 as being part of a Great Hall which John de Lewknor had commissioned before 1349; it had never been completed, possibly due to the Black Death, and has since been part of the farm.

The large white-fronted house opposite the church is probably the old rectory; note the older brick behind the Georgian façade. There is also a tidy Regency style house on the left past the post office. Leave a closer inspection of the pub for when you return from the walk!

ASTON HILL: This large sweep of beech-clad slope has been a crucial point of communication for centuries. The Icknield Way runs along its base and the London to Oxford Turnpike ran down it, not once, but twice, the original route being replaced in 1824. There was a station on the Watlington railway next to the Ridgeway, and now there is a BT repeater station on top of it. Yet these busy lines seem miles away as you wind up the old path through the pheasant-rich woods. It's easy to see why this was a favourite hiding place for highwaymen who used to make this entry to the Chilterns a fearful one.

WATLINGTON RAILWAY: As you head uphill from the B4009 look for a low ridge across the ploughed field. This is the old railway from Princes Risborough to Watlington which was closed in 1953 but has been restored as far as Chinnor and it is now suggested that Aston station should be reopened as part of a Park and Ride system to London!

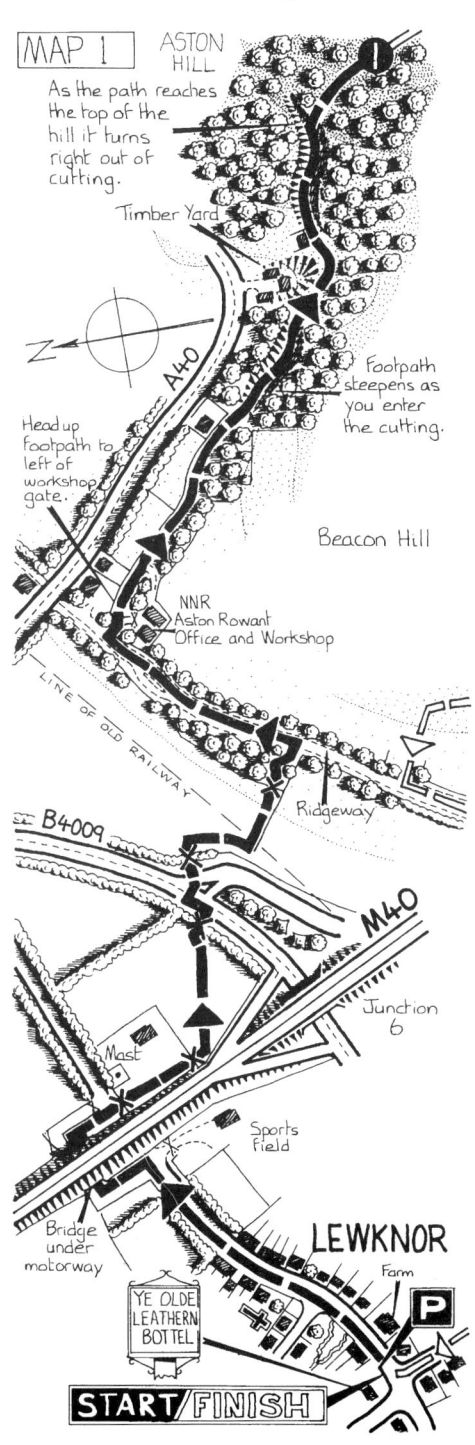

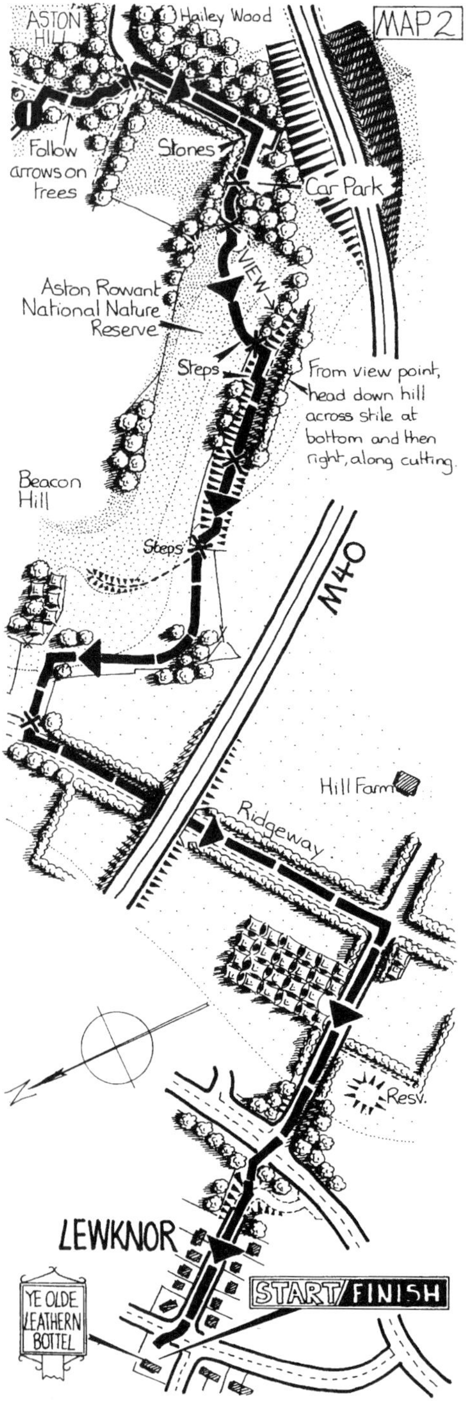

MAP 2

HAILEY WOOD: A positive spin off of the motorway was the discovery of ancient occupation. In Hailey Wood was found a settlement while further down before the Ridgeway passes under the M40 was a Saxon burial field; 39 cremation urns were uncovered!

ASTON ROWANT NATIONAL NATURE RESERVE: The first thing you will notice is the superb views over the Vale. Look a little closer to home and a circling bird of prey or grazing deer will probably catch the eye. Closer still and this open chalk downland will reveal a rich base of flora: orchids, candytuft, gentian and yellow wort flourish in their season; butterflies may add a final splash of colour to this pastoral picture.

> **REFRESHMENTS:**
> THE OLDE LEATHERN BOTTEL, High Street, Lewknor. Rambling old pub and inn. Telephone: 01844 351482.
> Next to the church there is a village shop which sells food and drinks.

Map labels:
ASTON HILL
Hailey Wood
Follow arrows on trees
Stones
Car Park
Aston Rowant National Nature Reserve
VIEW
Steps
From view point, head down hill across stile at bottom and then right, along cutting.
Beacon Hill
Steps
M40
Hill Farm
Ridgeway
Resv.
LEWKNOR
YE OLDE LEATHERN BOTTEL
START/FINISH

St Margaret's church

Walk 12
WEST WYCOMBE
Length 4 miles

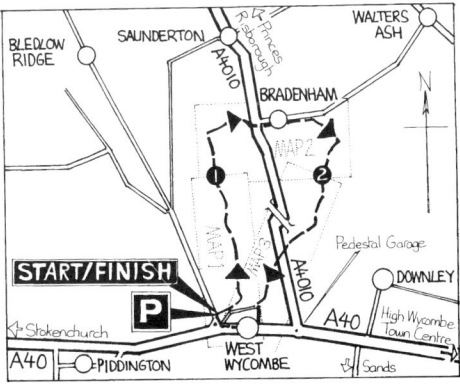

West Wycombe village.

GETTING THERE: From High Wycombe head out on the A40 towards Oxford. After a few miles you leave the town by the Pedestal Garage and keeping to the A40 head into West Wycombe village. At the far end is a right-hand turn signposted to Bledlow Ridge. Go up here and almost immediately on the left, just after a walled garden centre, is the car park.

INTRODUCTION: Two National Trust villages are the focal points of this walk. The imposing Georgian fronted buildings which tower over West Wycombe contrast with the humble cottages spaced out around the green at Bradenham. Here the picket fences and roses frame 'chocolate box' images

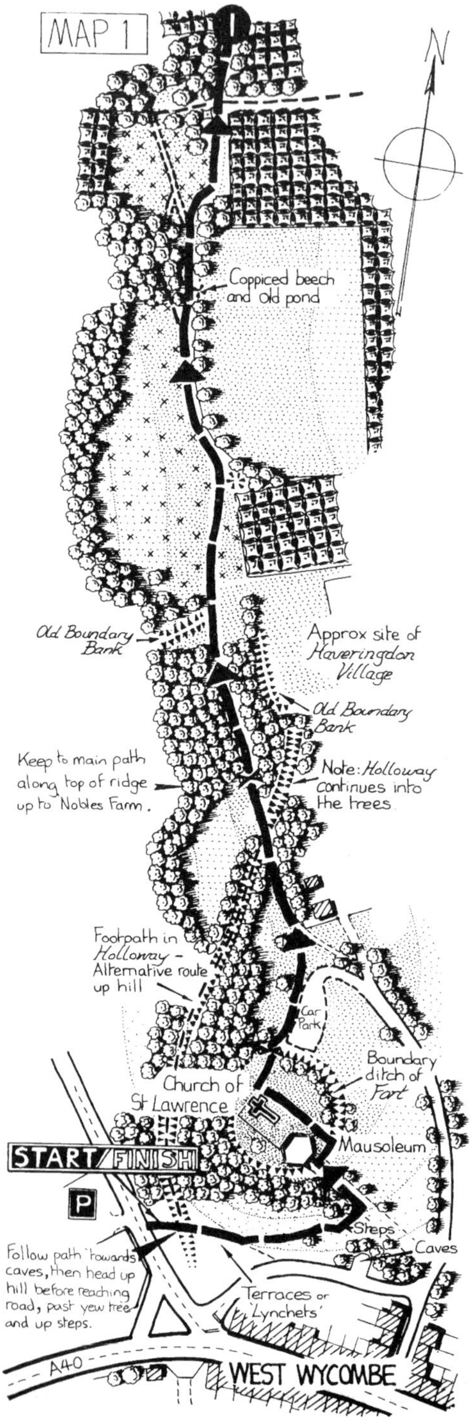

MAP 1

Coppiced beech and old pond

Old Boundary Bank

Keep to main path along top of ridge up to Nobles Farm.

Footpath in Holloway – Alternative route up hill

Approx site of Haveringdon Village

Old Boundary Bank

Note: Holloway continues into the trees.

Car Park

Church of St Lawrence

START/FINISH

P

Follow path towards caves, then head up hill before reaching road, past yew tree and up steps.

Boundary ditch of Fort

Mausoleum

Steps

Caves

Terraces or Lynchets

A40

WEST WYCOMBE

while at West Wycombe it is the houses of different shapes and sizes which leave the lasting impression. In between, the walk passes the famous church of St Lawrence with its golden ball and goes through the beech woods which cap the hills around the villages. There is more at the end of the walk than just a pint, with West Wycombe House and the unique caves worth making time for.

WEST WYCOMBE VILLAGE: The Iron Age fort on the hill above the village is testimony to the antiquity of the area although the earlier settlement was probably along the ridge and not in the valley below. The village today is a strung out collection of timber-framed and brick buildings of which the Church Loft with its 15th-century origins is the most notable. Look out for the mark of a cross on the east end of the frontage where it is said Roundheads removed the metal insert which once fitted here during the Civil War. There is also a cuff hanging from the west end which is from the old village stocks.

THE CHURCH OF ST LAWRENCE: Local legend has it that 'when they tried to build the church in the valley the foundations kept collapsing.

Then a mysterious voice suggested that they try at the top of the hill where they found success'. A more likely reason for its position is that the village it was built to

The cuff on Church Loft.

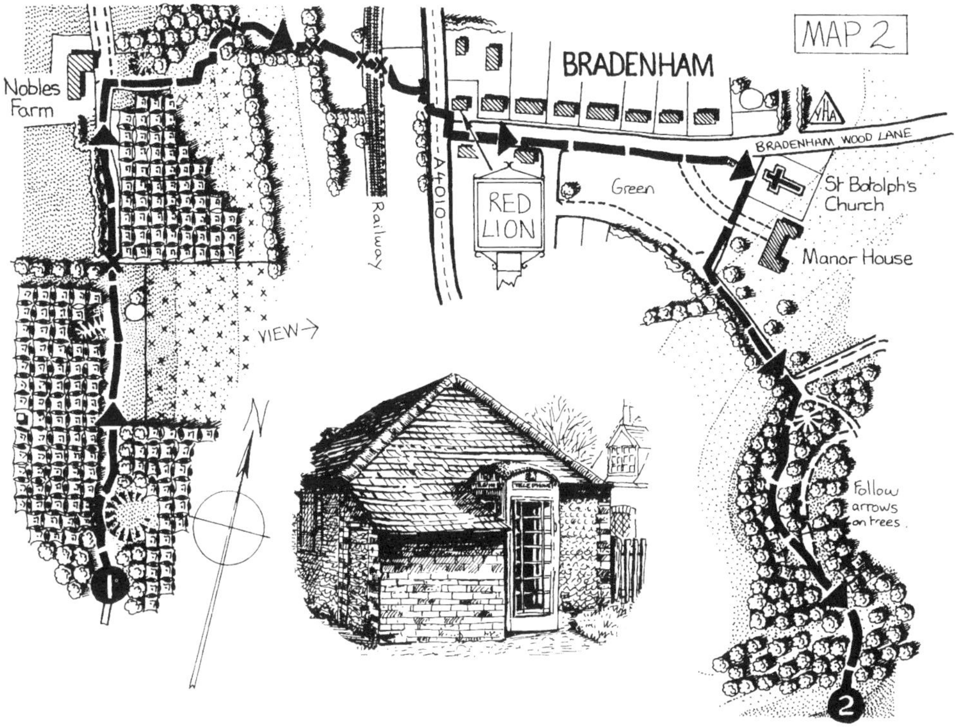

MAP 2
BRADENHAM
Nobles Farm
BRADENHAM WOOD LANE
YHA
St Botolph's Church
Manor House
Green
RED LION
A4010
Railway
VIEW→
N
Follow arrows on trees
1
2

serve was Haveringdon, a long forgotten settlement on the ridge, and not the later West Wycombe in the valley below. Although 12th-century in origin (notice the base of the tower and the chancel) the present building is a grand, classical edifice which was created by Francis Dashwood in the 1760s. Its most notable feature is the golden ball. Dashwood would invite his more adventurous friends to drink here, probably to steady their nerves!

MAUSOLEUM: Also built by Dashwood with funds left by George Doddington, a fellow member of the infamous Hell Fire Club (note his name along the cornice at the

View over Bradenham.

Red Lion
Old Park Boundary
Church
Manor

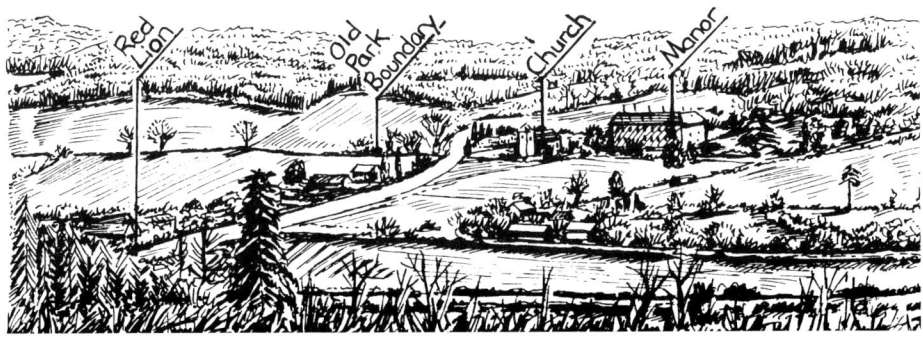

top). Within it are urns which were designed to hold the hearts of his friends including Paul Whitehead's which was placed there in 1775 with much ceremony, and then stolen in 1830.

HAVERINGDON: Although recorded in old documents there is nothing visible of what was probably only a small settlement except the old track in a holloway and earthworks.

BRADENHAM: Just off the busy Aylesbury road is this picturesque collection of cottages around a green which now serves as the village cricket pitch. Along its edge are some sarsen stones which have been dug up in the locality. Overlooking this is the old brick manor house which was the home of Isaac D'Israeli. A descendant of a Jewish family from Spain and Italy he was notable in his own right as an author. But it is his son Benjamin Disraeli, the Prime Minister (who seems to have anglicised his name), who will be best remembered, although he later moved to nearby Hughenden.

Before their time there was an Old Park here. The remains of its boundary banks can be traced north of the village and a site of medieval buildings has been discovered in the woods behind.

ST BOTOLPH'S CHURCH: At first glance a typical flint church but under the porch is a doorway surrounded by a Norman arch which is 900 years old. The decoration around the arch includes a depiction of St Botolph with flying swans and a church. Another secret it hides are the bells which have in their number two of the oldest bells in England.

WEST WYCOMBE CAVES: These man-made caves were excavated in 1758-63

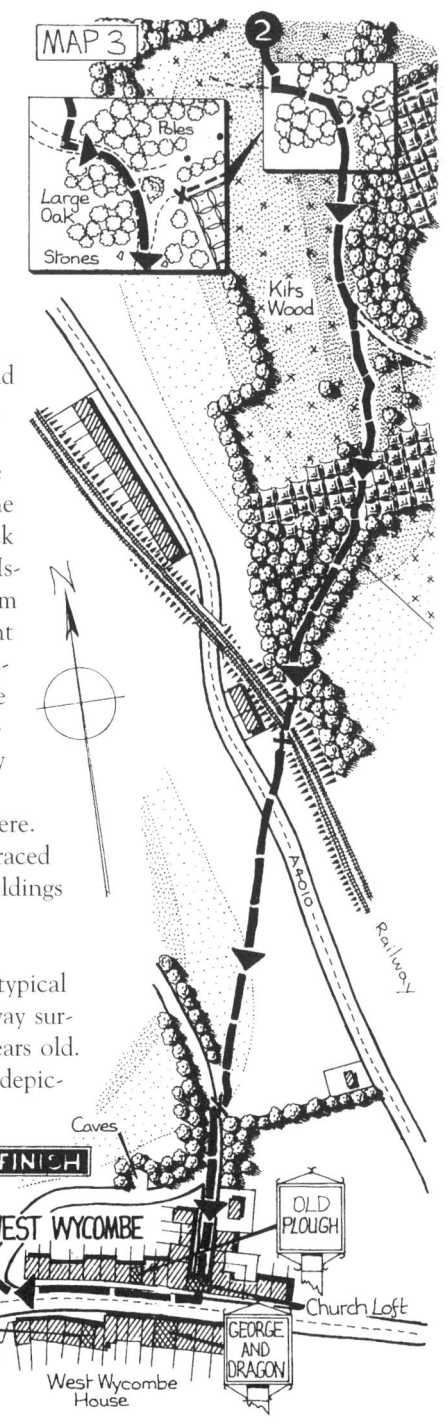

to supply material for the new road to High Wycombe. This was being financed by Francis Dashwood as part of a scheme to help local unemployment. There is a suggestion that earlier catacombs were incorporated in the digging but this and other stories mainly involving the Hell Fire Club probably have little foundation. The caves were restored and enlarged in the 1950s before they were opened to the public.

WEST WYCOMBE HOUSE: Originally a brick structure owned by Thomas Lewis, who on marrying a Dashwood gave the house to her brothers Samuel and Francis. The latter bought out the former in 1707 but it was his son, the 2nd Baronet, who rebuilt the house and gardens into what you see today.

SIR FRANCIS DASH-WOOD: The 2nd Baronet has been hailed as the 'Worst Chancellor of The Exchequer' while he held the post in 1762, but architecture was his first love. He gained a love for classical architecture while in Italy visiting among others Bonnie Prince Charlie, and he was instrumental in the first excavations of the Roman towns of Pompeii and Herculaneum. Despite all the work he did in West Wycombe he is best remembered for the Hell Fire Club (see Walk 20).

REFRESHMENTS:
THE RED LION, Bradenham. Ordinary looking but could be up to 400 years old. Open 11 am to 2.30 pm and 6 pm to 11 pm; no food Sunday and Monday evenings. Telephone: 01494 562212.
THE GEORGE AND DRAGON, West Wycombe. An 18th-century coaching inn with good food and beer. Open 11 am to 2.30 pm and 5.30 pm to 11 pm. Telephone: 01494 464414.
THE OLD PLOUGH, West Wycombe. Small doorway leads to a downstairs and upstairs bar with a garden at the rear. Open 11 am to 2.30 pm and 5.30 pm to 11 pm, all day on Friday and Saturday. Telephone: 01494 446648.
THE SWAN, West Wycombe. Tidy, unspoilt pub on High Street. Open 11 am to 2 pm and 5.30 pm to 11 pm. Telephone: 01494 527031.

West Wycombe

Walk 13
HIGH WYCOMBE
Length 3 miles

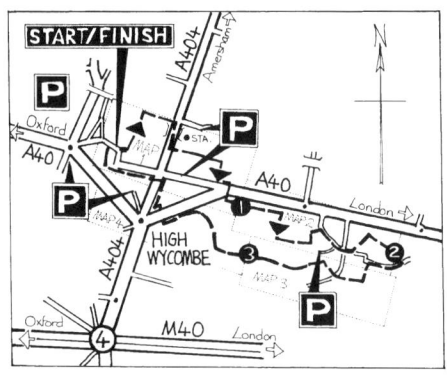

GETTING THERE: There are numerous car parks in the town centre which are well signposted from whichever direction you enter. These are all pay and display. An alternative place to park (but one which is very busy on Sunday mornings) is the free car park on the Rye. To get there head out of town on the A40 towards Beaconsfield and just after the first mini roundabout is a dark fence surrounding the cricket ground. Turn right at the end of this fence down Bassetsbury Lane and as the houses end on the right turn up the concrete road to the swimming pool. The car park is at the end past the tennis courts. If this is busy there is

usually space along Bassetsbury Lane.

As there are numerous places to park and hence to commence the walk I have not marked a starting point. Map 1 starts from the town centre as finishing here leaves plenty of opportunities for refreshment. Should you park next to the swimming pool then I would suggest that you pick up the walk on Map 2 so that food and drink is again towards the end of the circuit.

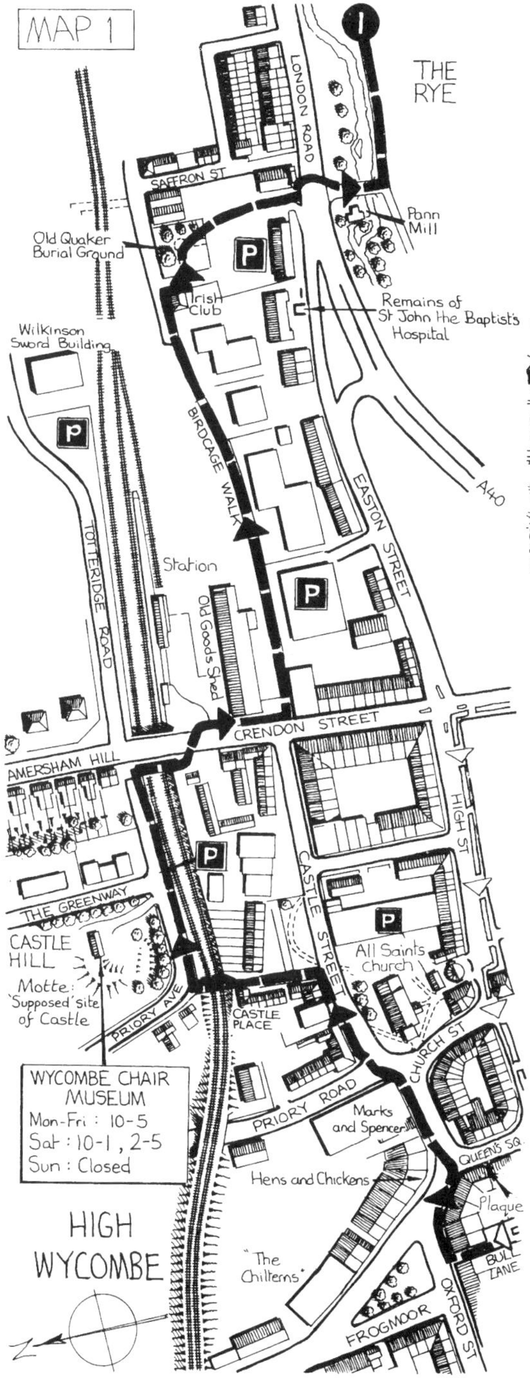

ST JOHN THE BAPTIST'S HOSPITAL

HIGH WYCOMBE: Numerous ancient finds confirm the presence of man since the Stone Age but the town did not start to take shape until medieval times when it was an important agricultural centre. It used to supply bread to the royal palaces in London and cloth for the tents in Edward I's Scottish campaign in 1296 (as in the film *Braveheart*). But it was the expansion of the furniture trade in the 19th century which shaped the town we see today.

HANNAH BALL: Above a travel agent's in Queen's Square is a plaque commemorating Hannah Ball who along with John Wesley founded the first Sunday school in the 1750s.

ALL SAINTS' CHURCH: A 13th-century building which originally had a central tower. This was replaced by

MAP 2

The spring and pool were originally one but were split in two by the railway.

Old Railway

Pool

Steps

Spring

OLD MILL

CHESTNUT AVE

KEEP HILL RD

Dairy

MARSH GREEN HOUSE

BASSETSBURY LANE

Mill

Cricket Ground

BASSETSBURY MANOR

HOLYWELL MEAD

Tennis Courts

RIVER WYE

P

Site Of Roman Villa

Flats

RYE MILL

LONDON ROAD

RIVER WYE

A40

Playground

THE RYE

Open Air Swimming Pool

the present west tower 200 years later, but you can still see the differing masonry where the former used to be. Opposite is the old priory, now shops. A workman fell into an old well associated with it when the site was being redeveloped in the 1970s.

CASTLE HILL: An old motte and bailey castle once stood in the gardens of what is now the local museum (similar to the Castle Tower site on Walk 8).

ST JOHN THE BAPTIST'S HOSPITAL: Not a medical hospital in the modern sense but a place for the relief of the poor or infirm. The set of parallel arches are the remains of the 12th-century hall. The hospital was closed in 1547 by the Crown but granted back to the town on the condition it should be a grammar school, which the building behind was until it was in turn resited up Amersham Hill early in the 20th century. Opposite are the remains of Pann Mill which was named after Roger De Panis and was working into the 1950s.

ROMAN VILLA: In 1722 workmen discovered a Roman mosaic with circles, squares, hearts and many curious figures. The villa dates from the 2nd century AD and was a grand house with 14 rooms and a large bath house. This theme has been continued as a swimming pool has now been built on the

BASSETSBURY MILL

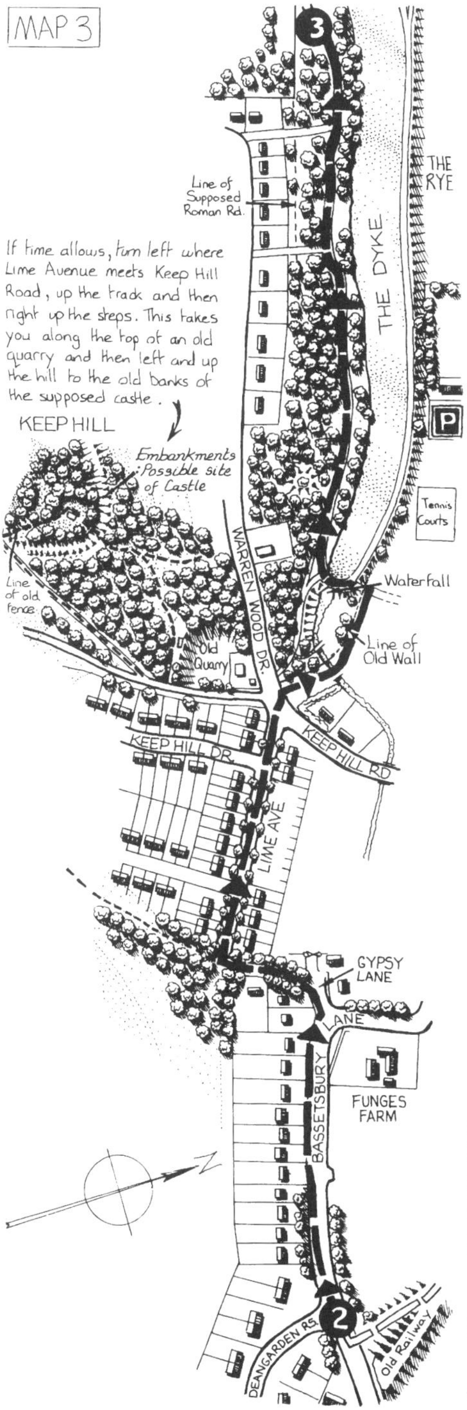

MAP 3

Line of
Supposed
Roman Rd.

If time allows, turn left where
Lime Avenue meets Keep Hill
Road, up the track and then
right up the steps. This takes
you along the top of an old
quarry and then left and up
the hill to the old banks of
the supposed castle.

KEEP HILL

Embankments
; Possible site
of Castle

Line
of old
fence.

THE RYE

THE DYKE

WARREN WOOD DR.

P

Tennis
Courts

Waterfall

Old
Quarry

Line of
Old Wall

KEEP HILL DR.

KEEP HILL RD.

LIME AVE

GYPSY
LANE

LANE

BASSETSBURY

FUNGES
FARM

N

2

DEANGARDEN RD

Old Railway

site. Curiously a mosaic studied just before the pool was built in 1954 is not the one discovered in 1722! Are there still more remains yet to be uncovered?

BASSETSBURY MANOR: In 1203 King John of Robin Hood fame granted half of his manor to Alan Basset. He didn't care much for the town and when he tried to syphon off more money than he was due, the locals rose against him. They won the right to the profits from the estate while he retained the right to collect dung from the streets!

The current manor house dates from the 1600s but was in a ruinous state by the 19th century. Local furniture man Fred Skull bought the house in the 1930s and completely renovated it. The porch at the front came from a building in Nottingham Market while some of the internal fittings came from the Old Quaker Meeting House in Crendon Lane (which was being widened into Crendon Street at the time). The mill at the rear has expanded from a core dating from the 16th century and included two sets of wheels and an inn at one point.

MARSH GREEN HOUSE: Originally believed to be a lodge for a larger house, this Gothic building has since been among other things a workhouse!

Waterfall, The Dyke.

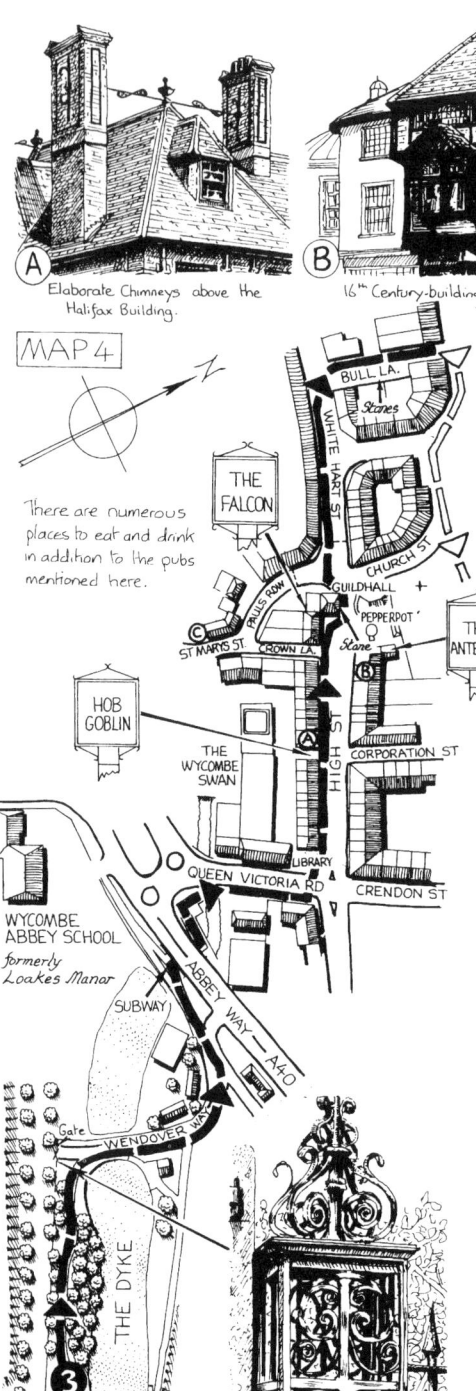

Elaborate Chimneys above the Halifax Building.

16ᵗʰ Century-building by the Shambles.

Old Furniture Factory on St Marys St.

MAP 4

There are numerous places to eat and drink in addition to the pubs mentioned here.

THE FALCON

HOB GOBLIN

THE WYCOMBE SWAN

WYCOMBE ABBEY SCHOOL
formerly Loakes Manor

SUBWAY

THE DYKE

OLD RAILWAY: The embankment you walk along here is the old Great Western line from Maidenhead to Wycombe. It was the first railway to reach the town and carried on to Risborough then west to Oxford. It wasn't until the 20th century that the new main line from Marylebone was built which used this original railway between Wycombe and Risborough before continuing north to Banbury. Despite being a useful link this old branch was closed between Wycombe and Bourne End in 1970.

KEEP HILL: In 1826, two labourers were throwing stones on the slope of Keep Hill when one flint 'the size of a swan's egg' split open revealing eleven gold coins. These were of late Iron Age date and similar hollow flints have been found in Surrey and Kent where they appear to have been used as money boxes!

The earthworks around the hill could be even older but are also believed to be associated with a castle on the site.

THE RYE AND DYKE: The Rye is an ancient tract of land onto which the people of the borough had the right to bring cattle, up until the 1920s. The only problem was that grazing was only permitted in daylight hours so every evening the animals were herded back to sheds often at the rear of shops and buildings in the town centre. It was a daily sight to see cattle up and down the High Street but by 1927 this dangerous combination of cow and car brought about the change of the Rye from pasture to recreational use.

In 1643 while the town was a garrison for the Parliamentary forces, a surprise attack was launched by Royalists. This so-called 'Battle of Wycombe Rye' is claimed to have accounted for 1,200 lives. Unfortunately, with scant evidence and with books giving varying details about the event, it's more likely it was just a local skirmish that has been blown out of proportion.

The Dyke appears to be a watercourse formed when it was part of Loakes Manor in the 18th century although there is some suggestion that the retaining bank was in part an ancient barrow as a skeleton was found in it! The old line of wall by the waterfall was possibly the boundary before the Dyke became part of the Rye in the 1920s.

WYCOMBE ABBEY: This famous girls' school is formed around a building dating back to the 17th century when it was known as Loakes Manor. It was remodelled in the current Gothic style in 1804 by Wyatt and renamed at the same time. The school took over the site nearly a hundred years later.

WENDOVER WAY: The now concrete road leading up to the elaborate gates was formed in 1923, dividing the Dyke into two with the smaller west section still within the school. It was named after Lord Wendover who had been killed in the First World War.

HIGH STREET: Take a look above the shop fronts as you walk along and you will notice Victorian and Georgian buildings, and one clearly Tudor. The Guildhall at the head of the road was built in 1757 and three years later the 'Shambles' appeared opposite. The latter was criticised at the time as being poorly built and spoiling the view of the church! Notice a number of stones set in the pavement, one by the Guildhall and a few up Bull Lane. These are long forgotten boundary stones on which boys' heads were hit when performing the ancient ceremony of 'Beating the Bounds'!

All Saints church, Wycombe

Walk 14
WATLINGTON
Length 5 miles

Watlington

GETTING THERE: From junction 6 on the M40, take the B4009 to Watlington. Upon entering the town take the first turn left up Hill Road and then the second turn right into the car park.

INTRODUCTION: In a bid to increase traffic on the Watlington Railway in the early part of the 20th century the area was promoted as being rich in bluebells. I had forgotten how true this still is until I walked through Lower Deans Wood early in May. Even if you cannot visit at this time of year you will get pleasure from stunning views from two points, a surprising oasis in the middle of

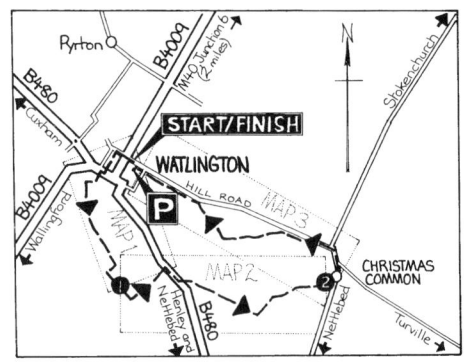

fields and the ancient market town itself.

WATLINGTON: The ancient aura the rambling brick façades give is justified. An Iron

Age burial place of a chieftain's wife was found here, the town was noted in the Domesday Book as having five mills and there was once a castle. On the site of this now stands the church and most of the houses would have at one time stood around it, but by the 14th century the town had started to shift to its present position centred around the Town Hall. This was built in 1665 by Thomas Stonor (see Watlington Park) and served as a grammar school and market as well. The shops and buildings off the Market Square mainly date from the 17th and 18th centuries. At this time the town was notorious for numerous inns and pubs, until the 19th century when a local Methodist bought up six and closed them all down! The arrival of the railway in a field north of the town had little effect and Watlington today seems to have avoided large developments and bypasses which have marred similar places.

Notable buildings to look out for include the silver and red Georgian 'High Street House'. Also of special note is the yellow Granary with its mushroom-shaped stone legs. These helped keep rats and moisture out when it was used to store grain.

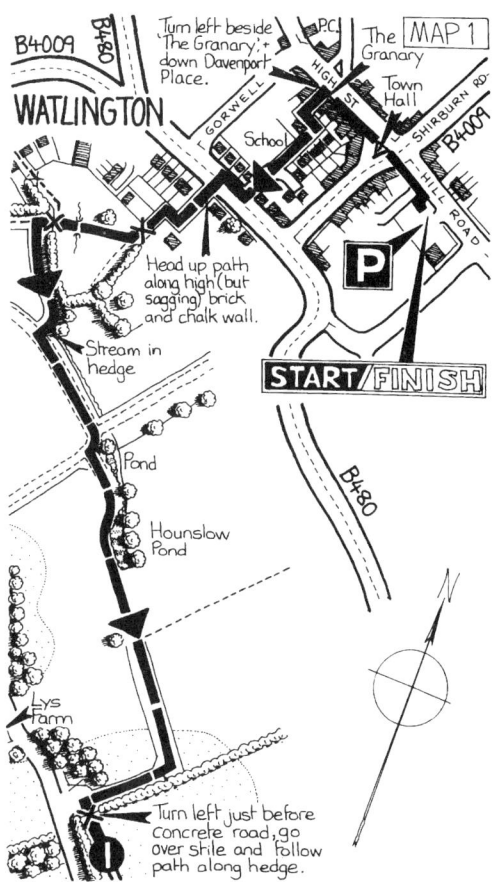

HOUNSLOW POND: When the water which soaks through the porous chalk of the hills hits the clay level below, it runs along it and out of the ground in the form of springs. These can be quite a way from the hills themselves, and it comes as a surprise to find this one in the middle of a field. Hounslow Pond (so named on an old map) is rare in that it has, or has been, formed into a small lake and is home to an isolated collection of flora and fauna.

WATLINGTON PARK: William Stonor bought the freehold to the site in 1632 from Charles I and built an H-shaped house and

park on it. His son Thomas Stonor still had sufficient funds available to build the Town Hall in 1665. The house was then sold in 1753 to John Tilson who constructed the present building with the old house being used as the kitchen block. These remains were finally demolished in the 1950s along with various extensions returning the façade to its original five bays width.

LOWER DEANS WOOD: This otherwise unexceptional beech woodland comes to life in spring with a profusion of bluebells. Try and time your walk for the end of April and early May, though if not you will still

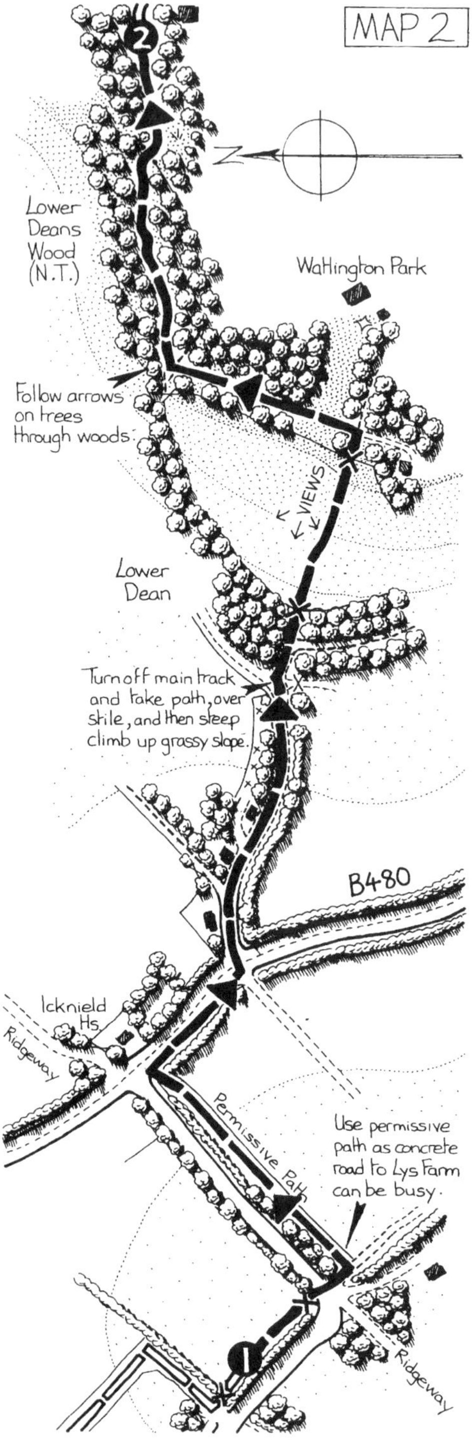

MAP 2

Lower
Deans
Wood
(N.T.)

Watlington Park

Follow arrows
on trees
through woods

VIEWS

Lower
Dean

Turn off main track
and take path, over
stile, and then steep
climb up grassy slope.

B480

Icknield
Hs.

Ridgeway

Permissive Path

Use permissive
path as concrete
road to Lys Farm
can be busy.

Ridgeway

Spring in Lower Deans Wood.

find the silent and still air below the high beech canopy a refreshing change from the fields before.

CHRISTMAS COMMON: A string of houses along the crossroads on top of Watlington Hill. The peculiar name is of unknown origin but may come from the holly which grows in the area, although there was also a 'Christmas' family living at the farm of the same name – which one came first? There was probably a medieval park here with the hamlet only forming later to serve the Stonors' house and the surrounding land. The farm and pub date back to the 17th century; the other houses are later with the row of Forestry Commission buildings very modern indeed!

WATLINGTON HILL: This 680 ft high peak commands excellent views along the escarpment and out into Oxfordshire. The hill itself is covered on its south side by a notable forest of yews. The remainder has

View over Watlington.

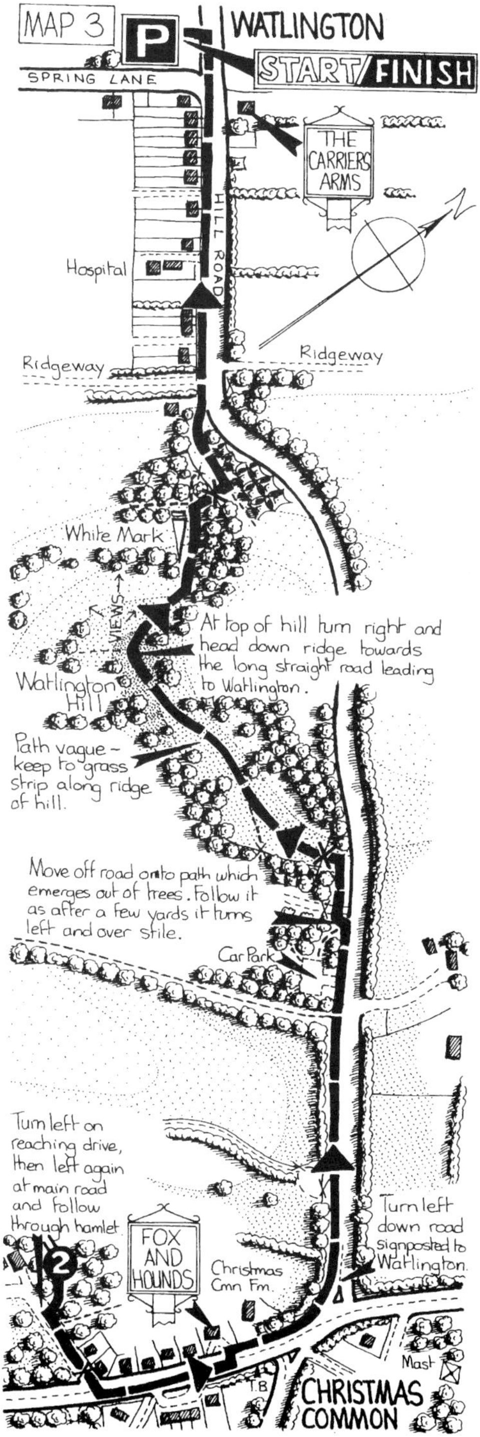

dogwood, hawthorn, whitebeam and the wayfaring tree (you can also see these in the rich hedgerows along the Ridgeway earlier).

THE WATLINGTON MARK: This is not an ancient cutting shrouded in mystery like the Whiteleaf Cross, but an 18th-century folly. The 270 ft high mark was cut on the orders of Edward Horne of Greenfields in 1764 and was meant to represent an obelisk.

RED KITES: If you are lucky, you may catch sight of this rare bird that has recently made a home in these parts. It is one of our largest birds of prey, growing to twice the size of a kestrel. It can easily be identified by its deeply forked tail. It may also be possible to spot one on Walk 15 – Ibstone.

REFRESHMENTS:
THE CARRIERS ARMS, Watlington. Telephone: 01491 613470.
THE FOX AND HOUNDS, Christmas Common. Telephone: 01491 612599.

MAP 3 P WATLINGTON
START/FINISH
SPRING LANE
HILL ROAD
THE CARRIERS ARMS
Hospital
Ridgeway   Ridgeway
White Mark
VIEWS
Watlington Hill
At top of hill turn right and head down ridge towards the long straight road leading to Watlington.
Path vague – keep to grass strip along ridge of hill.
Move off road onto path which emerges out of trees. Follow it as after a few yards it turns left and over stile.
Car Park
Turn left on reaching drive, then left again at main road and follow through hamlet
FOX AND HOUNDS
Christmas Cmn Fm.
Turn left down road signposted to Watlington.
Mast
T.B.
CHRISTMAS COMMON

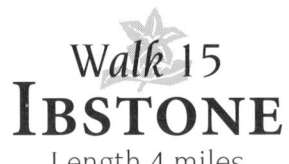

Walk 15
IBSTONE
Length 4 miles

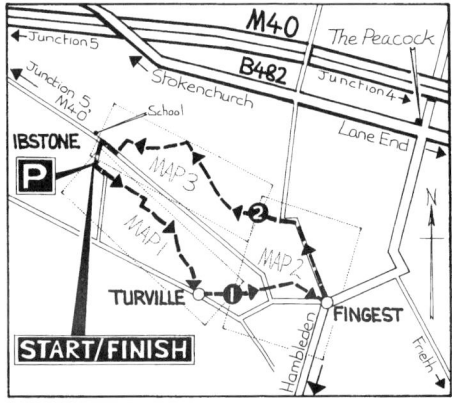

St Bartholomew's church

GETTING THERE: From Stokenchurch and junction 5 on the M40 head over the motorway towards Ibstone. Carry on this road through the long village for about 2 miles until you pass the small school on your left. Almost immediately, as the road appears to fork, turn right down a narrow tree-lined lane. There are some spaces on the left-hand side of the road to park in before the lane makes a sharp left turn. The walk starts by heading down this lane towards that sharp bend.

Alternative starting points: There are places to park in Turville and Fingest but these become busy even on weekdays. If you can park in either of these villages you will find refreshment at the end of the walk – well worth consideration when you see the Chequers and Bull and Butcher!

INTRODUCTION: Three Norman churches act as cornerstones for this walk through the best loved valley in the Chilterns. Beech woods, grassy slopes and fields surround the villages of Turville and Fingest nestling in the valley bottom overlooked by the much filmed windmill. Ibstone on the other hand has stretched away from its church leaving it isolated on the hillside beside the old manor house and a yew of even greater antiquity.

St Nicholas church, Ibstone

ST NICHOLAS CHURCH: Hidden behind trees is this modest building covered in a patchwork of plaster. Underneath the humble exterior is a Norman church almost 900 years old! Note the semi-circular top to the south, and, now blocked, north doorways, details unique to a building of this date. If open take a look at the interior of the church and don't forget the ancient yew tucked around the west end, its heavily ribbed trunk indicating a ripe old age.

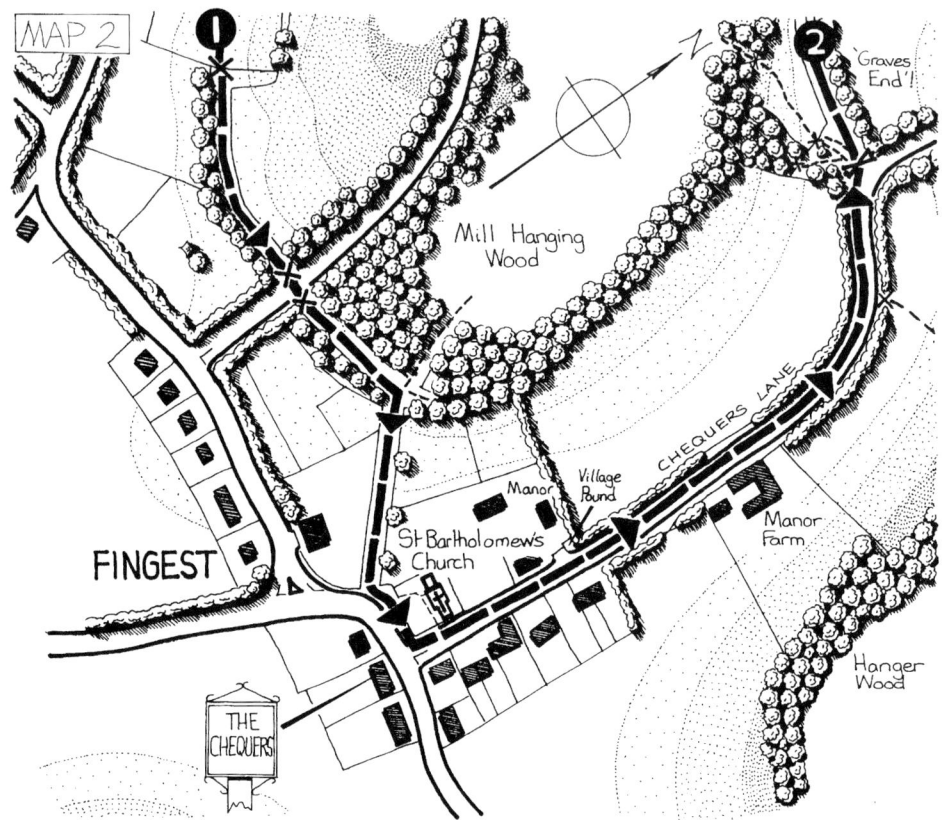

TURVILLE: With its green surrounded by cottages, church and pub, Turville has attracted tourists and cameras alike. Most of the houses are 17th to 19th-century timber-framed or brick and flint buildings, with the most notable being the Old Vicarage. It has a late 17th-century core with a Regency-style front over the garden. Note the odd little turret on top of the barn, a neat 20th-century addition.

ST MARY'S CHURCH: Although Norman parts remain, most of what you see is about 700 years old, with the brick aisle at the rear being an 18th-century carbuncle. Inside is a stone coffin discovered during restoration

which dates to the 13th century and around the south doorway are supposed pilgrim crosses which were cut into the masonry for those lost in battle.

COBSTONE MILL: This smock mill dates back nearly 200 years although there has been one here since 1633. Now a residence, it was in the film *Chitty Chitty Bang Bang* and looks down on the village featured in *The Vicar of Dibley*.

FINGEST: The Bishops of Lincoln had a so-called palace here which they probably used as a hunting lodge and the remains of its last incarnation were visible up to the 19th cen-

St Bartholomew's church, Fingest

tury. A story associated with this tells how one such Bishop, Henry De Burghersh, gained a licence in 1330 to empark 300 acres including land which belonged to the villagers. The infuriated locals could do nothing! But then after his death one of his squires saw an apparition in the woods of the late Bishop dressed as a huntsman; this pleaded with the startled man to return the land that had been taken otherwise the spectre was condemned to eternity amongst the trees. The squire related the story to the relevant department in Lincoln that dealt with ghosts, and a canon was promptly dispatched to oversee the removal of the boundaries and release the Bishop from his rather tame penance!

The village today has a small number of pretty houses and an 18th-century pub but all is dominated by the huge church tower in the middle.

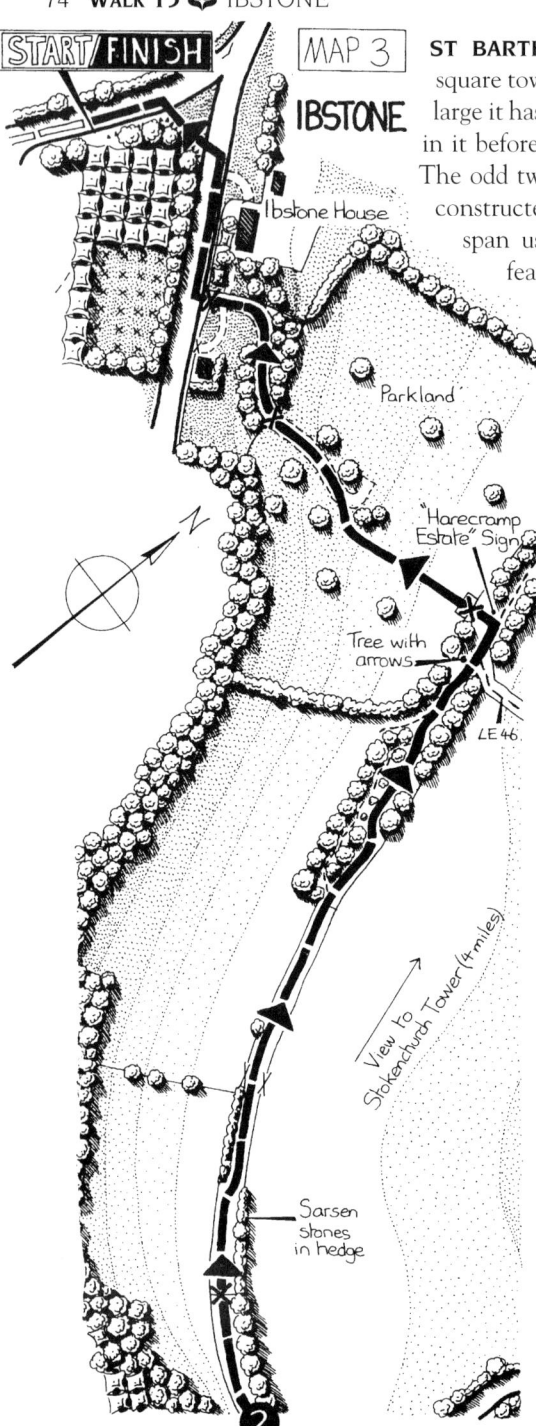

ST BARTHOLOMEW'S CHURCH: The huge 27 ft square tower is getting on for 900 years old and is so large it has been suggested that the congregation sat in it before the main body of the church was built! The odd twin roof is an example of what was often constructed where the distance was too great for one span using older heavy tiles. Another notable feature is the painted plaster exterior which gives it a welcoming warm tone unlike most local churches where this has been stripped off to reveal stark grey flints.

IBSTONE: Although the village would once have stood around the church it has since drifted further along the ridge towards Stokenchurch. At our end the church and Manor Farm remain, while as you climb out of the valley you pass through the old parkland which surrounds Ibstone House. This stuccoed, castellated building is more than 200 years old, but is mostly obscured by the attractive gardens which surround it.

RED KITES: Keep an eye open above you for this rare bird of prey which has recently made a home in this area (see also Walk 14). It is twice the size of a kestrel or crow and has a forked tail.

REFRESHMENTS:
THE CHEQUERS, Fingest. The attractive 15th-century beamed interior and huge garden are just two of its features. Open 11 am to 3 pm and 6 pm to 11 pm. Telephone: 01491 638335. THE BULL AND BUTCHER, Turville. Another picturesque pub dating back 400 years and also with excellent food. Open 11 am to 3 pm and 6 pm to 11 pm. Telephone: 01491 638283
    There is also The Fox in Ibstone about halfway back towards the motorway junction.

Walk 16
DENHAM
Length 3 miles

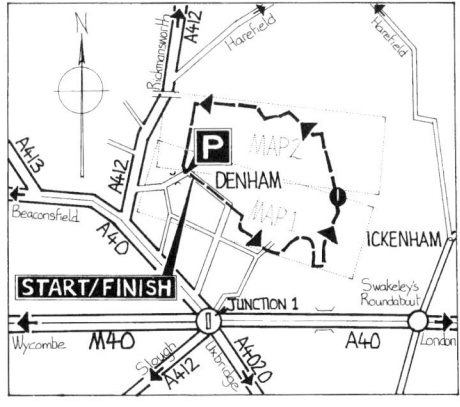

Denham village

GETTING THERE: From junction 1 of the M40 head north along the A40 towards Gerrards Cross and at the first set of traffic lights turn right up the A412. Take your first right down Village Road, signposted to 'Denham Village' and park either alongside the brick wall just before the little bridge or further on around the green.

INTRODUCTION: What a surprise it is to turn off the noisy Rickmansworth road and to suddenly become enshrouded in this tranquil village from a bygone age. This walk meanders past some ancient brick and timber houses and then through the more recently created Colne Valley Park. The circular route continues along the Grand

Union Canal with the black and white lock perfectly framed by the overhanging trees. You return through the woods that surround a peaceful stretch of the River Colne and then along the railway, entering the village

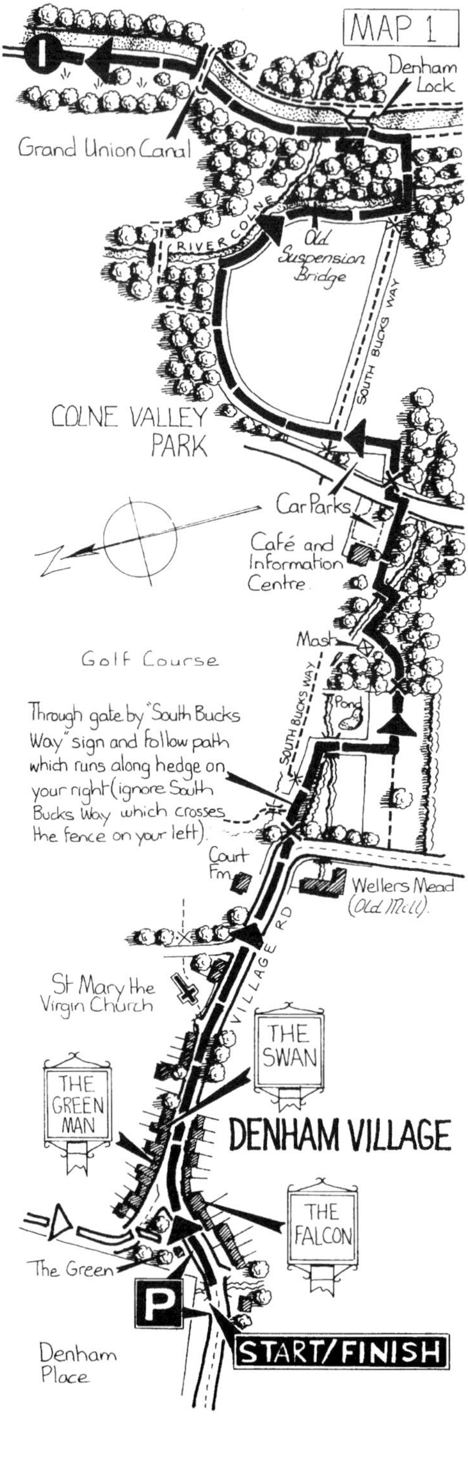

MAP 1

Denham Lock

Grand Union Canal

Old Suspension Bridge

RIVER COLNE

SOUTH BUCKS WAY

COLNE VALLEY PARK

Car Parks

Café and Information Centre

Golf Course

Marsh

SOUTH BUCKS WAY

Pond

Through gate by "South Bucks Way" sign and follow path which runs along hedge on your right (ignore South Bucks Way which crosses the fence on your left).

Court Fm

Wellers Mead (Old Mill).

VILLAGE RD

St Mary the Virgin Church

THE SWAN

THE GREEN MAN

DENHAM VILLAGE

THE FALCON

The Green

P

Denham Place

START/FINISH

by the high brick walls of Denham Place.

DENHAM VILLAGE: Denham is sandwiched between two large houses. Denham Place, surrounded by a high brick wall which you notice as you enter the village, was the home of the Vansittart family in the 1600s. It is a mainly 18th-century building with grounds laid out by Capability Brown (his real name was Lancelot but he gained his nickname from telling his clients that their gardens had 'capabilities of improvement'). At the other end near the River Colne is Denham Court, the grounds of which have since formed a golf club and the country park you walk through.

In between, the idyllic scene is created by a mix of timber-framed cottages and later brick houses including the imposing Falcon which dominates the green. The church is a pleasantly set 15th-century building with next to it a fine Georgian house, finished with a set of Dutch gables. Just after is the highly decorative side of Cedar Cottage with below it a line of memorial stones fixed to the wall!

Denham lock

REFRESHMENTS:
There are three pubs in Village Road, all full of character, food and good beer!
THE FALCON, open 11 am to 3 pm and 5.30 pm to 11 pm; no lunches on Sunday. Telephone: 01895 832125.
THE GREEN MAN, open 11 am to 3 pm and 5.30 pm to 11 pm. Telephone: 01895 832760.
THE SWAN, open 11 am to 11 pm. Telephone: 01895 832085.
There is also a teashop next to the cottage at Denham Lock. Open 10 am to 7 pm Easter to October, 10 am to 4 pm November to Easter.

START/FINISH   MAP 2

Denham Place

Denham Station

DENHAM VILLAGE

Golf Course

GRAND UNION CANAL: The Grand Union Canal was only formed as a company in 1929, long after the railways had sealed the fate of the canals and they themselves were losing out to the car. Before it had been a collection of eight separate waterways, the most important part being the main line from London to Braunston in Northamptonshire. This was the Grand Junction Canal which was built in the early 19th century with wide locks to encourage the use of more economical 70 ton barges. Unfortunately other companies stuck with their narrow canals and this helped speed up their demise when they faced competition from the railways. Then in 1932 the newly merged Grand Union Canal launched a massive Government backed programme to widen the whole length to Birmingham and although it helped unemployment the job was never completed and commercial traffic slowly died. Thankfully the peaceful waterway has been preserved for leisure.

This length at Denham is fed by the river Colne so you will notice that the water is unusually clear and full of life.

Just before the railway bridge, turn left along Permissive Horseride.

RIVER COLNE

Follow path which meanders through wood until crossing the river again.

Widow's Cruise Covert

RIVER COLNE

RAILWAY: This was another late starter, being the last main line built in England, early in the 20th century. When the railwaymen came to Denham the golf club on the other side of the A412 refused them the land unless they built a station for them. Denham Golf Club still has a wooden halt serving it today!

Grand Union Canal

Before reaching railway bridge, turn left down steps beside map, and then right shortly after at crossroads of paths.

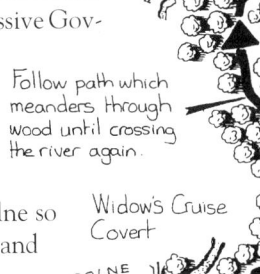

Walk 17
NETTLEBED
Length 4½ miles

Westwood Manor Farm

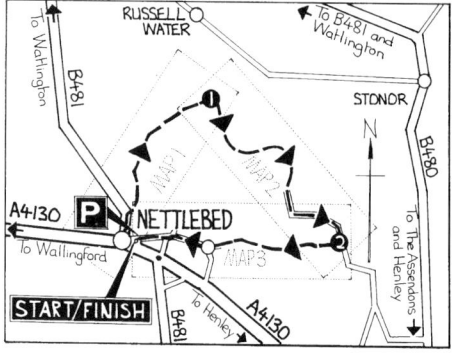

GETTING THERE: Nettlebed is on the A4130, Henley to Wallingford road. Once in the village look for the junction with the B481 to Watlington, and just on the Henley side of this turning is an island with a shelter. Park on the road that circles around this or along the side road.

INTRODUCTION: It is a great characteristic of the Chilterns that you can find remote, timeless places only a short distance from busy towns. Bix Bottom is one such location; only a few miles from Henley but more than a few years distant in time. The winding narrow road that is the only vehicular access to the valley helps maintain this isolation. This attraction has been further enhanced by the Warburg Reserve which protects the wooded slopes with a diversity of flora and fauna that can be appreciated by all. In contrast, Nettlebed has fine Georgian buildings which date back to the days when it was an important coaching stop on the London road, and fortunately two pubs survive to serve you on your modern day travels.

With the addition of the old kiln, a ruined church and the remote, rolling hills this unique walk is full of surprises on every turn.

NETTLEBED: The name refers to the plant though thankfully they are not a significant feature of the landscape today. The church is a typical Victorian flint building but its roots are unusually long. St Birinus was sent by the Pope to preach gospel to the more remote parts of Britain and became friends with Cynegils, Saxon king of the Whitta. His daughter was betrothed to St Oswald but the marriage could not proceed unless Cynegils embraced the Christian faith. St Birinus was therefore called on to baptise the king and in return was granted land to set up the first Saxon Bishopric which included establishing a church at Nettlebed in AD 640.

The main road which the church overlooks is the old route from Oxford and Wallingford to London and it was turnpiked in 1736. Although some of the buildings along the High Street are older most were built or refaced in this prosperous period.

NETTLEBED COMMON: Today a large tract of trees and scrub cover the remains of the brickmaking industry which dominated this landscape well into the 20th century. This local trade can be traced back to the 14th century when 35,000 bricks were made for Wallingford Castle, and 50 years later for Stonor House. By the 1800s this was a flourishing business with numerous kilns and works spread over a smoky terrain of pits. The coppiced trees which still survive in large numbers in the surrounding woods were grown to fuel the fires which carried on burning up to the Second World War.

The remaining kiln, from where you start the walk, dates from the 18th century and

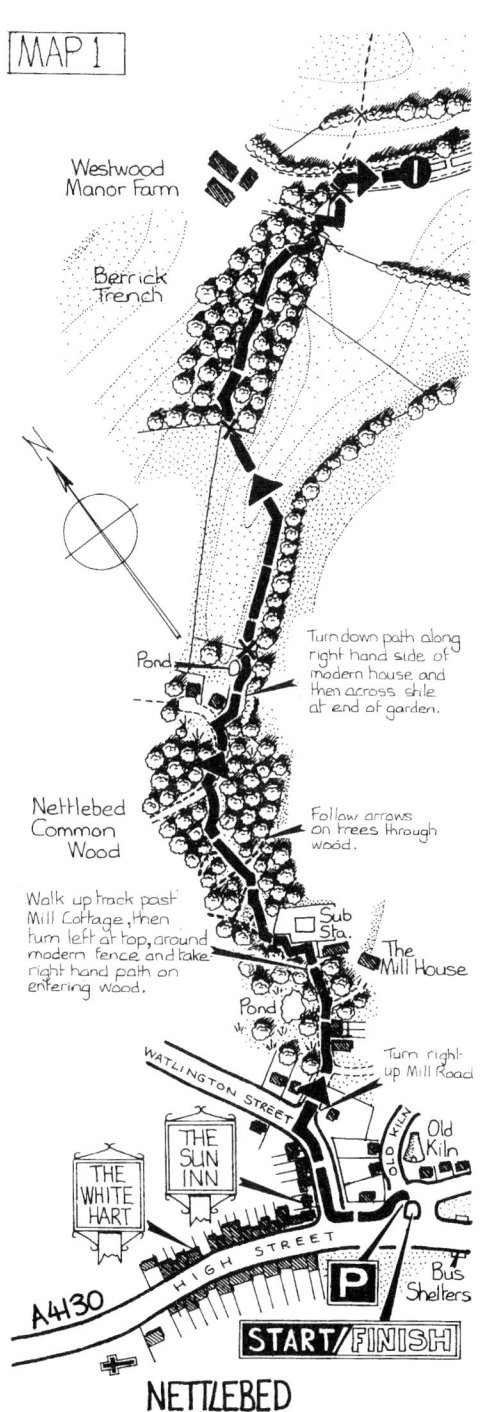

MAP 1

Westwood Manor Farm

Berrick Trench

N

Pond

Turn down path along right hand side of modern house and then across stile at end of garden.

Nettlebed Common Wood

Follow arrows on trees through wood.

Walk up track past Mill Cottage, then turn left at top, around modern fence and take right hand path on entering wood.

Sub Sta.

The Mill House

Pond

Turn right up Mill Road

WATLINGTON STREET

THE SUN INN

Old Kiln

OLD KILN

THE WHITE HART

HIGH STREET

A4430

P

Bus Shelters

START/FINISH

NETTLEBED

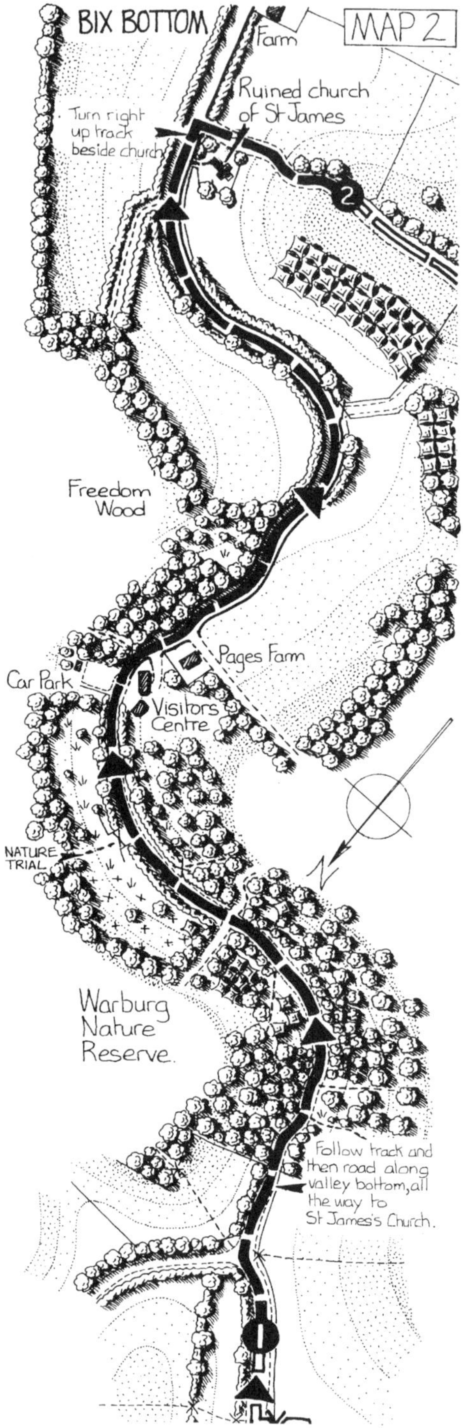

BIX BOTTOM
Farm MAP 2

Ruined church
of St James

Turn right
up track
beside church

2

Freedom
Wood

Pages Farm

Car Park

Visitors
Centre

NATURE
TRIAL

Warburg
Nature
Reserve.

Follow track and
then road along
valley bottom, all
the way to
St James's Church.

was used until 1938. It looks a little out of place surrounded by modern housing but along with the ponds and pits on the common behind it serves as a reminder that the Chilterns was a working landscape.

WARBURG RESERVE: This is the largest of the Berks, Bucks and Oxon Naturalists' Trust's nature reserves and the beech woodland and open spaces encourage a wide diversity of wildlife. You don't have to know your flora and fauna to appreciate the variety. Beech is dominant but interspersed with oak, yew, birch, pines and firs. There is also some coppicing and examples of traditional hedge laying. Muntjac and fallow deer, grass snakes, lizards and adders can be seen while the numerous wooden boxes set low on tree trunks are for dormice! The open spaces between the woods also encourage flowers of which 15 different species of orchid are the highlight. For further information contact the visitors' centre on 01491 642001.

The ruins of Bix church

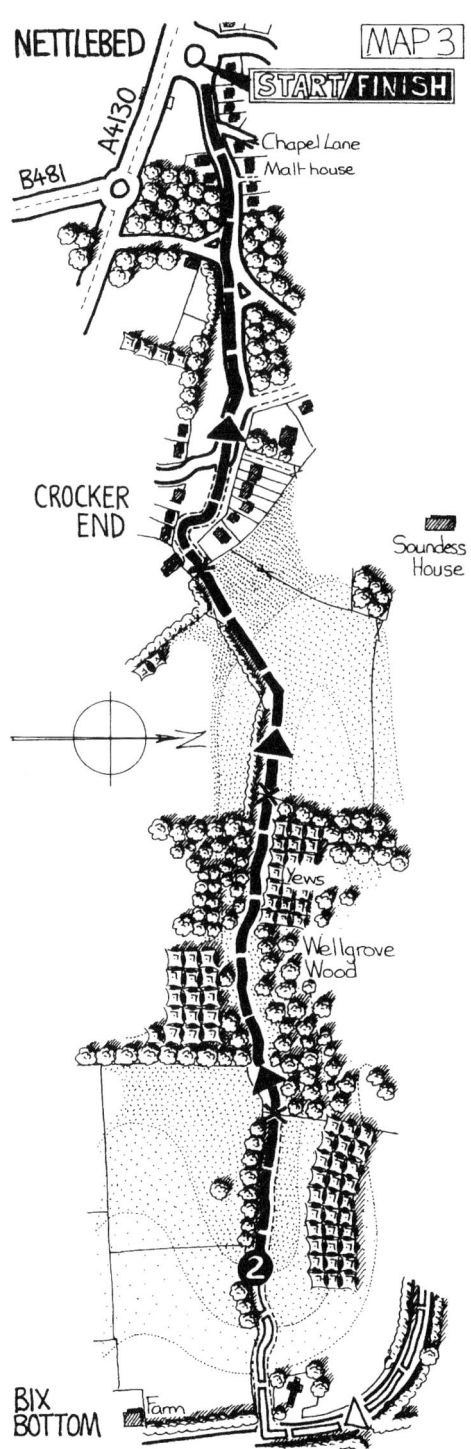

BIX CHURCH (ruins): It's rare in this part of England to come across a ruined church, but the crumbling masonry seems quite appropriate in this forgotten valley. Only the shells of the nave and chancel survive with a Norman-style arch in between the two. It probably dates from the 12th century when there was a larger settlement here. By the last century Bix had progressed up the hill to its current site on the Wallingford to Henley road. A new edifice was erected to serve it and the fitments from the old church were removed there.

CROCKER END: A tidy set of 17th to 19th-century cottages, now much extended, around an elongated green strip. Flemish brickmakers are known to have settled here in the 15th century as records at Stonor mention 'Les Flemyngges' in an order for bricks. Better known is Nell Gwynn, the mistress of Charles II, who it is said lived for a time at nearby Soundess House. Some maps mark a spot in the grounds called Nell Gwynn's Bower.

PUDDLESTONE: You may have noticed the odd-shaped concrete block on the island as you started the walk. These stones have in fact been fused naturally millions of years ago. Why they are here is a mystery but it is alleged that they were used by prehistoric man as route markers. There is another one at The Lee (see Walk 5).

REFRESHMENTS:

THE SUN INN, Watlington Street. Telephone: 01491 641359.

THE WHITE HART, High Street. Open all day. Telephone: 01491 641245.

There is also a village shop next door to the Sun Inn.

WELL END
Length 5 miles

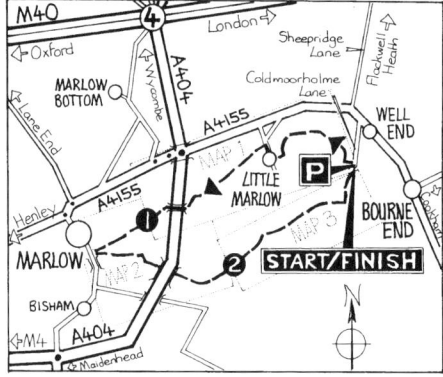

The riverside at Marlow.

GETTING THERE: From junction 4 on the M40 take the A404 south towards Marlow and Maidenhead. Turn off at the first junction and go left down the A4155 towards Bourne End. Follow the road for a mile or so and then just as you go past the 30 mph and Well End signs turn right down Coldmoorholme Lane. Keep along the lane, past the Spade Oak pub, then round a bend and the car park appears on your right.

INTRODUCTION: A walk of contrasts, from the lakes of the old gravel works to the oasis of Little Marlow, and from the historic cen- tre of Marlow to the tranquillity of the Thames. The first part of the walk follows the track which once linked the two com-

MARLOW [MAP 1]

Globe
Business
Park

FIELDHOUSE LANE

OSBORNE RD

SAVILL WAY

Housing
Estate

Marlow Bypass

Footbridge

A404

Westhorpe
House

THE
QUEENS
HEAD

Gravel
Workings
Access Road

Village
Pound

THE
KINGS
HEAD

Manor Hs.

LITTLE
MARLOW

SCHOOL LANE

Footbridges

Gravel
Workings

A4155

START/FINISH

P

Spade Oak
Pit

Spade
Oak

WELL
END

From car park head
back up lane past
Spade Oak pub and
then turn left through
gap in hedge just
after gate. This path
runs parallel with
the lane until
crossing a tiny
bridge. you veer
left through the trees
and emerge into a
field. Turn left and
keep to the path which
runs along the fence.

munities, then the circular route returns along the river which made Marlow into the bustling town of today. The stretch along the river is spectacular in all seasons. Try it on a warm summer's day and then on a misty winter's morning!

LITTLE MARLOW: This antique island amongst a sea of gravel pits hangs onto its shape despite the waves of progress lapping at its edges. The major building is the Manor House, hidden behind high walls, 17th-century in origin with a dovecot in the garden. There is an old village pound opposite the Queens Head and a large box-framed house next to the church. St Mary's has 12th-century windows and a pleasant mix of later styles (the church is open between 2 pm and 4 pm on Sundays). The thriller writer Edgar Wallace is buried in the churchyard.

GRAVEL EXTRACTION: Gravel is made of mainly flints worn into round stones by, in this case, the Thames which once flowed across these fields. Since the early 1930s these meadows have been dug leaving large pits most of which are now water filled and used for leisure. As these sites are nearly exhausted gravel pits in places like Beaconsfield have been used, once on the route of the ancient river Thames when it used to flow into the Wash!

WESTHORPE HOUSE: 18th-century house which can be viewed at close quarters from the footpath. It is now a management centre.

MARLOW: Originally a busy agricultural outlet onto the Thames which was saved from depression by a blossoming leisure industry and close proximity to London.

MARLOW BRIDGE: The original

St Mary's church, Little Marlow

crossing was from the end of St Peters Street but this was replaced in 1832 by the suspension bridge. So impressed was one of the contractors that he named his daughter Charlotte Suspensiana Clifford! Its designer, William Tierney Clark, also built a bridge in Hungary linking Buda with Pest (hence Budapest). When the bridge was repaired in the 1960s they peeled off so much road spoil that they used it to resurface the path from Little Marlow to the town centre!

ALL SAINTS' CHURCH: 'Mould around the pews' due to regular flooding was one of the reasons for the old church to be rebuilt in 1830. This was remodelled only 50 years later into its present form, although rough brickwork under the south windows shows that this work was never completed.

MARLOW PLACE: An early 18th-century house which was supposedly built for the Prince of Wales. In the Second World War it was used as a factory for vital aircraft components. During this time a tunnel was uncovered reviving the legend of a secret passage under the Thames!

THE OLD PARSONAGE: Probably the oldest domestic building in the area, with 14th-century origins. Notice the two stone-traceried windows which look out of proportion with the low rambling façade.

ST PETER'S ROMAN CATHOLIC CHURCH: This church of 1845 was designed by Pugin whose other works include the Houses of Parliament. Its main point of interest is the mummified hand of St James the Apostle which is stored within!

Quarry Wood Hall

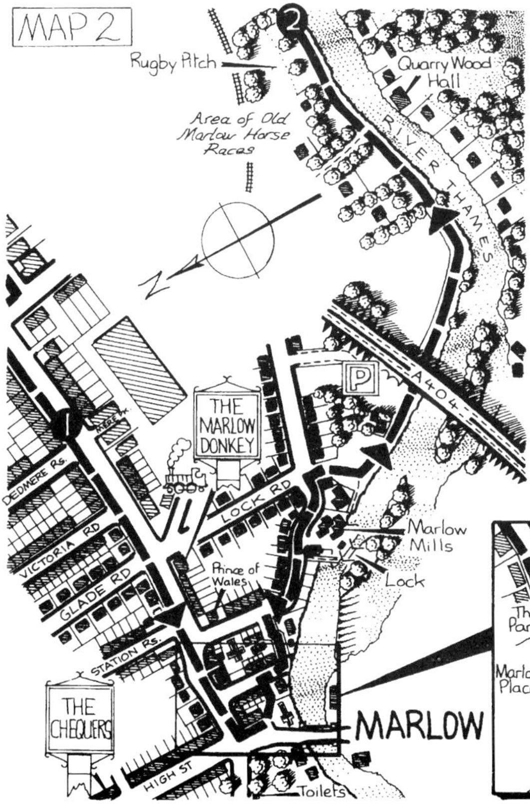

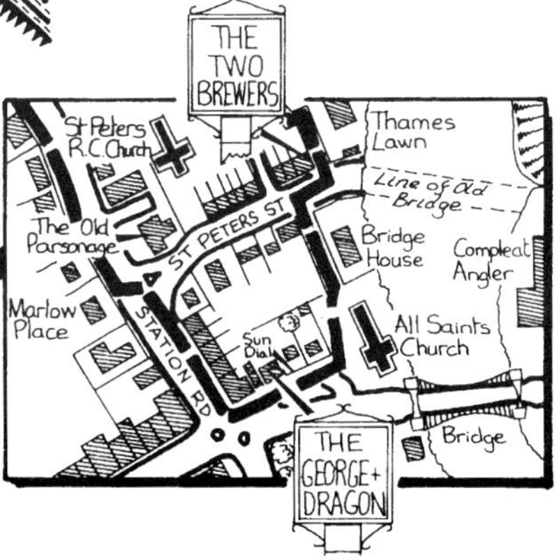

MAP 2

Rugby Pitch

Quarry Wood Hall

Area of Old Marlow Horse Races

RIVER THAMES

N

THE MARLOW DONKEY

P

A404

DEDMERE RD.

VICTORIA RD.

GLADE RD.

LOCK RD.

Prince of Wales

Marlow Mills

Lock

The Old Parsonage

STATION RD.

THE CHEQUERS

HIGH ST

MARLOW

Toilets

THE TWO BREWERS

St Peters R.C Church

The Old Parsonage

Marlow Place

ST PETERS ST

STATION RD.

Sun Dial

Thames Lawn

Line of Old Bridge

Bridge House

Compleat Angler

All Saints Church

Bridge

THE GEORGE + DRAGON

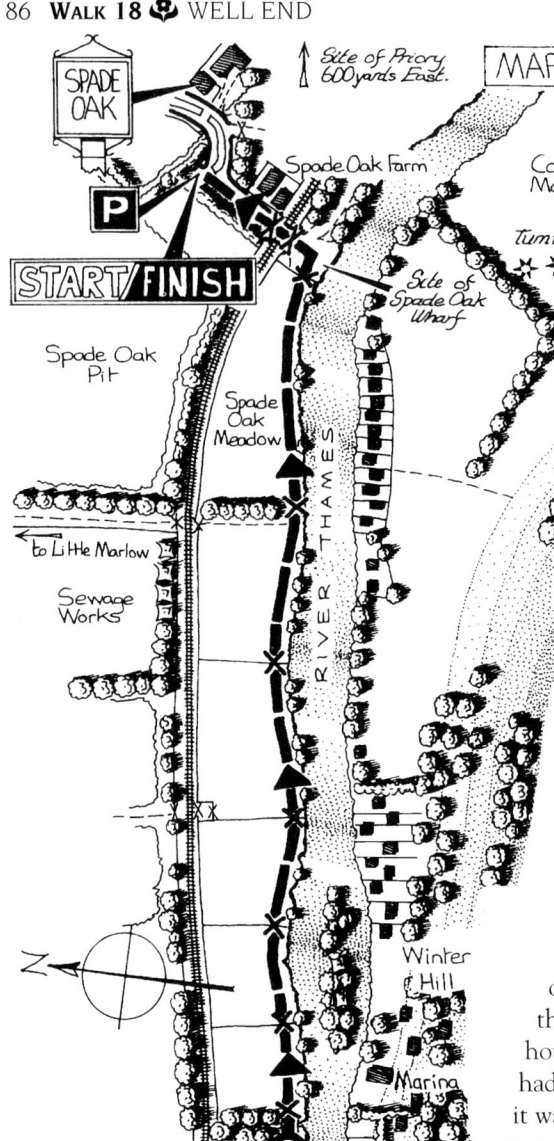

QUARRY WOOD HALL: Built in 1901, this fine example of Edwardian Gothic has entertained such guests as Virginia Woolf and Noel Coward.

OLD RACECOURSE: Marlow once had a famous race course which was located where the rugby pitch is today. It lasted from 1752 until closing finally in 1847.

SPADE OAK: There is no sign today of the old wharf although the ferry was still running up until 1956.

COCK MARSH: On the opposite side of the Thames is a flat area of meadow preserved by the National Tust. Within its bounds are a set of tumuli dating back a possible 5,000 years.

ST MARY'S NUNNERY: About ¼ mile away from Spade Oak is the site of an old nunnery rediscovered when the site was being redeveloped for housing in 1900. It was never large but had its own church and cloisters. When it was dissolved in 1536 it only had four nuns!

REFRESHMENTS:

THE SPADE OAK, Coldmoorholme Lane, Well End. Bar food and restaurant accompany good beer. Open 11 am to 11 pm. Telephone: 01628 520090.
THE KINGS HEAD, Church Road, Little Marlow. Characterful pub with home cooked food and good beer. Open 11 am to 3 pm and 5.30 pm to 11 pm. Telephone: 01628 484407.

THE QUEEN'S HEAD, Pound Lane, Little Marlow. Unspoilt local. Open 12 noon to 3 pm and 5.30 pm to 11 pm. Telephone: 01628 482927.
There are numerous pubs and places to eat in Marlow; particularly notable is the Two Brewers where parts of *Three Men in a Boat* were written.

BURNHAM BEECHES
Length 4 miles

Burnham Beeches

HOW TO GET THERE: From Junction 2 on the M40, head down the A355 towards Slough and after a few miles enter Farnham Common. Just past a small park on your left and as you approach the main shopping parade, turn right down Beeches Road. Cross the road at its end, enter Burnham Beeches on Lord Mayor's Drive and follow this road all the way through the woods until reaching the T-junction at the other side. Turn left and the parking space is immediately on your right, just before the Grenville Lodge.

INTRODUCTION: Beech woodland can become monotonous, but this is a spectacular exception to that rule. This is a walk for all seasons with the ever-changing colours

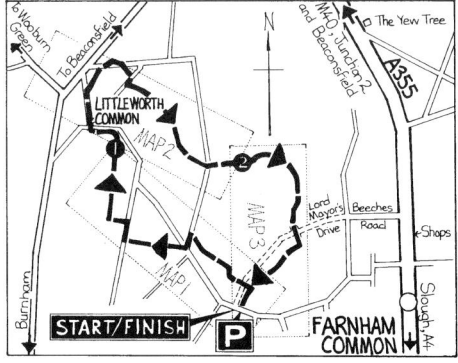

from spring through to autumn above, while the twisted and gnarled trunks below create shapes on a bleak winter landscape. In contrast, the silver birch trees on Littleworth Common are light and airy, which allows a wide range of flora to enhance the woodland floor.

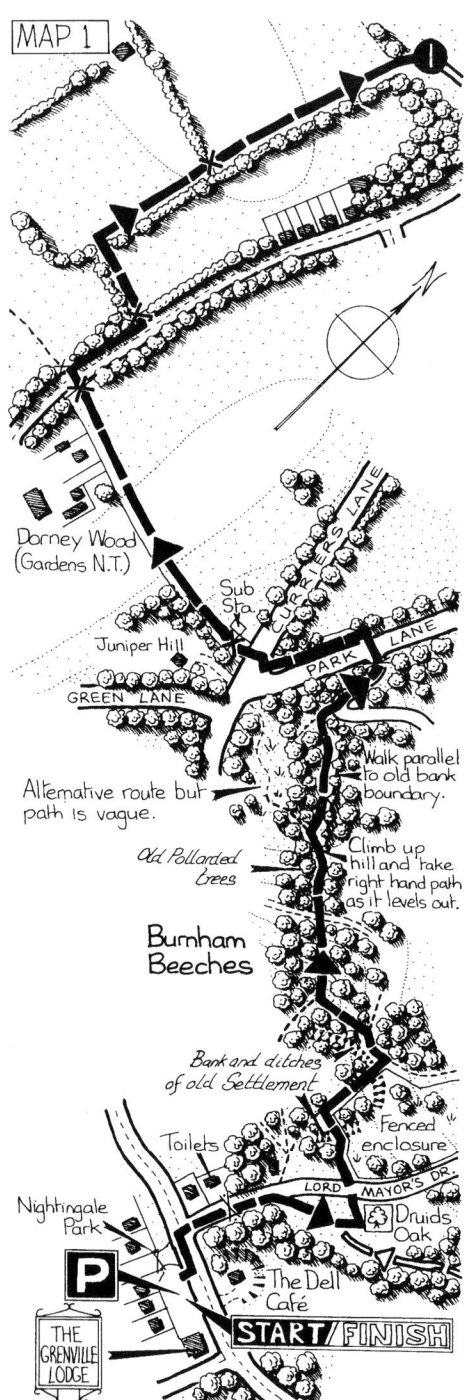

MAP 1

Dorney Wood
(Gardens N.T.)

Sub Sta

Juniper Hill

GREEN LANE

Alternative route but
path is vague.

Old Pollarded
trees

Burnham
Beeches

Bank and ditches
of old Settlement

Toilets

Nightingale
Park

THE
GRENVILLE
LODGE

COURTIERS LANE

PARK LANE

Walk parallel
to old bank
boundary.

Climb up
hill and take
right hand path
as it levels out.

Fenced
enclosure

LORD MAYOR'S DR.

Druids
Oak

The Dell
Café

START/FINISH

In addition you pass the country residence of the Foreign Secretary, four pubs, a rare woodland stream and remains of man's occupation that predates even the oldest trees.

BURNHAM BEECHES: A remarkable remnant of ancient woodland which, thanks to early preservation, has repelled the wave of suburbia knocking at its door. When the estate was being sold in 1878 the London Corporation purchased the wooded part and since then has enhanced it with new planting and roads for access to make the landscape we see today.

The view back in 1878 would have been very different though. The southern end was common land and therefore open for grazing with a scattering of pollarded trees. Most of the woodland around the start and finish of the walk has grown since.

Pollarding trees here is first recorded back in the 16th century. It was done by cutting the trunk above the reach of the grazing animals to encourage it to grow many thin branches. These were then cropped at regular intervals and used for firewood, fencing etc. This was continued until the 1820s but since then the huge weight of the uncropped branches has twisted the trunks into the strange contorted shapes which are now such a feature of the woods.

DRUIDS OAK: Pollarded trees can be very old, but older still is the Druids Oak. Approximately 350 years old, its name comes from oak's traditional association with Druids and does not apply to this particular tree.

SETTLEMENT: A circular bank and ditch to the west of Druids Oak of unknown date. It is most likely to be an old farmstead or just an animal enclosure.

DORNEY WOOD: The house and gardens were given to the National Trust in 1942, the former for use by a Secretary of State while the latter can be viewed on limited days of the year, by written permission!

LITTLEWORTH COMMON: This once open common land is now covered in a pleasant silver birch plantation. Bracken and moss cover the floor while one of the ponds which watered livestock remains by the Blackwood Arms. Three pubs stand on the sides of the triangle of land, each surrounded by old workmen's cottages mainly 18th and 19th-century in date. The parish church of St Anne is a red-brick Victorian building although it is linked with Dropmore, the large house to the west of here.

St Anne's church

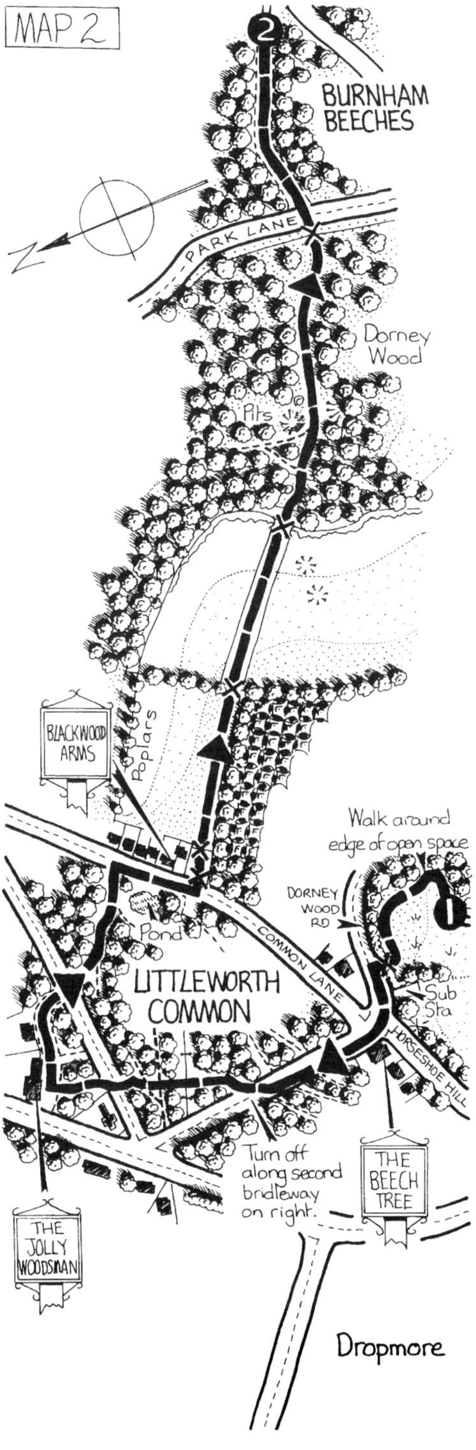

MAP 2

BURNHAM BEECHES

PARK LANE

Dorney Wood

Pits

Poplars

BLACKWOOD ARMS

Walk around edge of open space

DORNEY WOOD RD.

COMMON LANE

Pond

LITTLEWORTH COMMON

Sub Sta

HORSESHOE HILL

Turn off along second bridleway on right.

THE BEECH TREE

THE JOLLY WOODSMAN

Dropmore

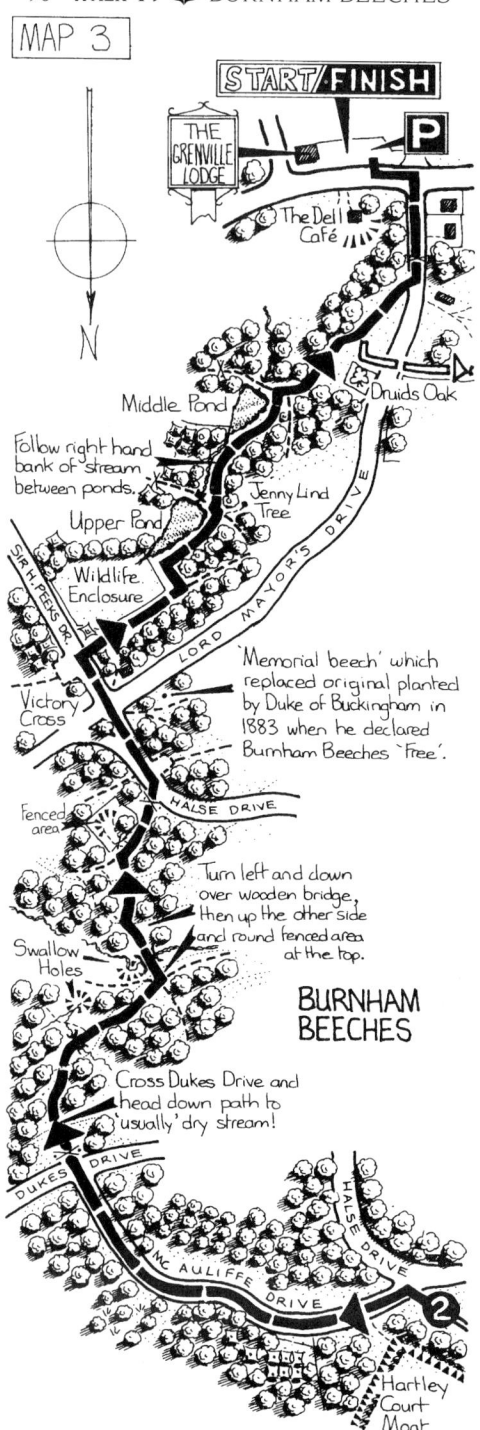

MAP 3

START/FINISH

THE GRENVILLE LODGE

P

The Dell Café

Middle Pond

Druids Oak

Follow right hand bank of stream between ponds.

Upper Pond

Jenny Lind Tree

N

Wildlife Enclosure

Victory Cross

'Memorial beech' which replaced original planted by Duke of Buckingham in 1883 when he declared Burnham Beeches 'Free'.

Fenced area

HALSE DRIVE

Turn left and down over wooden bridge, then up the other side and round fenced area at the top.

Swallow Holes

BURNHAM BEECHES

Cross Dukes Drive and head down path to 'usually' dry stream!

DUKES DRIVE

McAULIFFE DRIVE

HALSE DRIVE

2

Hartley Court Moat

HARTLEY COURT MOAT (also known as Hardicanute's Moat or Harlequins Moat): The dry moat covered in scrub and small trees once surrounded a farmstead dating from the 12th-14th centuries. The banks would have had fences and with the ditch would have protected the house from deer and swine. The surrounding woods, recorded in 1266 as 'Hertelgh' was ploughed up in the 1630s but with the later agricultural depression part of it returned to what is now called Egypt Woods.

MIDDLE AND UPPER PONDS: Both were man-made by the damming of the stream to form ponds for sheep dipping when this was open common land. Today the Upper Pond is one end of a reopened enclosure to encourage animals while the little woodland stream draws you down to the more secluded Middle Pond.

JENNY LIND TREE: Born in 1820, Jenny Lind was a famous soprano of her day who was known as the 'Swedish Nightingale'. She used to sit under a gnarled beech tree on this very spot and to commemorate the centenary of her death a new one was planted here in 1987.

REFRESHMENTS:
THE BEECH TREE, Dorney Wood Road. No food on Sundays. Telephone: 01628 661328.
THE JOLLY WOODMAN, Littleworth Road. At its heart, three old woodsman's cottages, possibly 16th-century. Open 11 am to 11 pm. Telephone: 01753 644350.
THE BLACKWOOD ARMS, Common Lane. Idyllic looking pub with the fastest changing range of beers in the country! Open 11 am to 2.30 pm and 5.30 pm to 11 pm. Telephone: 01753 642169.
THE GRENVILLE LODGE, Hawthorne Lane. Single bar with nightclub attached and large garden. Open 11 am to 11 pm. Telephone: 01753 643227.

Walk 20
MILL END
Length 6 miles

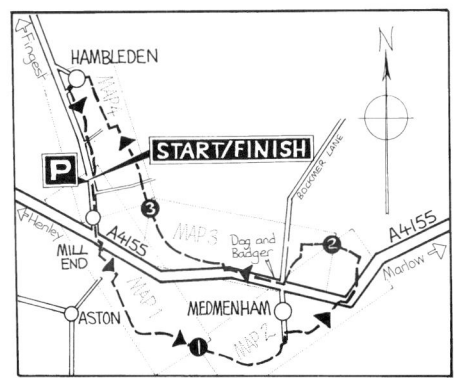

St Mary's church

GETTING THERE: From Marlow town centre take the A4155 towards Henley and follow it for approx 4 miles. After passing the
Dog and Badger and the Westfield turning,
the road twists and turns and then enters
the few houses and farm of Mill End. Take
the main right-hand turn signposted to
Hambleden and after a few hundred yards
turn left into the car park.

INTRODUCTION: This walk takes you
through two different landscapes influ-

Rosehill Wood

MAP 1

Culham Court

Pond

White thatched House

RIVER THAMES

A4155

Site of E-Shaped Roman Villa

MILL END

Mill End Farm

Marina

Hambleden Mill

Footpath on weir

Lock

Yewden Manor

Yewden Farm

Greenlands

START/FINISH

P

Site of Roman Villa (excavated 1911)

Culham Court

enced by the estates of Hambleden and Danesfield. The red-brick buildings in the village and around the fields of the former contrast with the ornate, white houses of the latter. On the way you pass through Thameside meadows overlooked by grand houses and return over open hills with commanding views. Both villages on the route have quiet lanes, rambling cottages and pubs to be discovered, though Hambleden will seem familiar as it has been the backdrop for numerous period dramas.

MILL END AND THE ROMAN VILLAS: This Thameside extension of the Hambleden parish is a collection of houses with a farm and mill on what was a busy site in Roman times. In 1911 the site of a large villa was excavated revealing an extensive complex with grain storage and furnaces for drying. These were probably to supply grain to Londinium. Greater mystery surrounds the 97 infant burials found in the foundations and precincts; a strange custom possibly involving the unwanted pregnancies of slave women!

Another villa site has been revealed by aerial photography beside the Thames. This E-shaped building has been confidently assigned to the same period although it bears more resemblance to a Tudor house. Nothing above ground can be seen of either villa but all the finds are now in the County Museum.

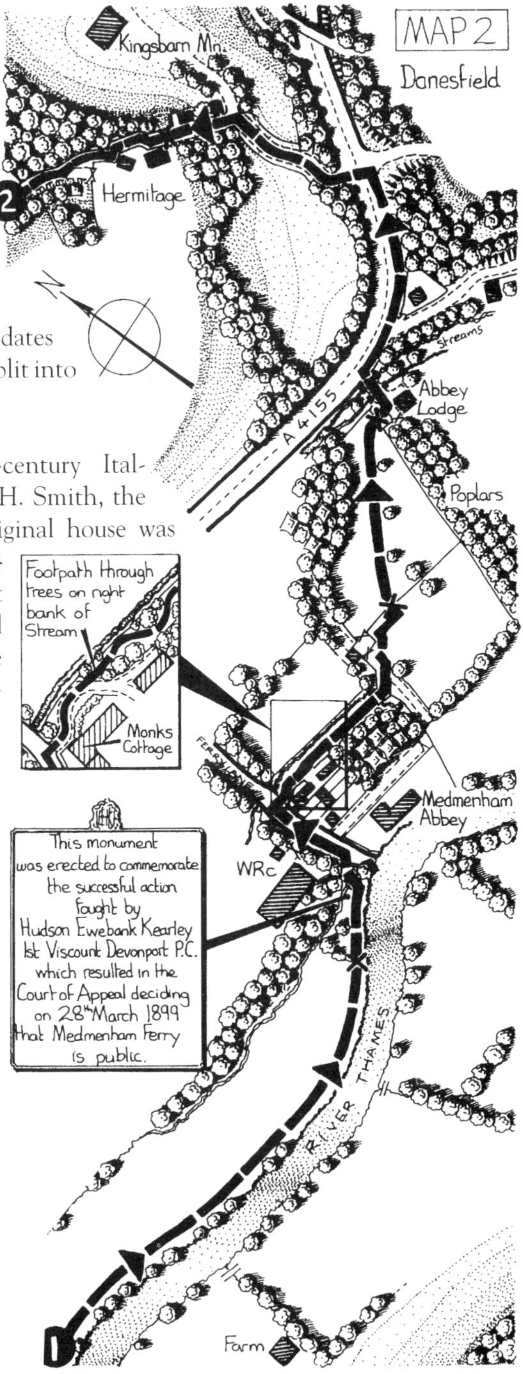
MAP 2
Danesfield
Kingsbarn Mn.
Hermitage
2
Streams
A 4155
Abbey Lodge
Poplars
Footpath through trees on right bank of Stream
Monks Cottage
FERRY LANE
Medmenham Abbey
WRc
This monument was erected to commemorate the successful action fought by Hudson Ewebank Kearley 1st Viscount Devonport P.C. which resulted in the Court of Appeal deciding on 28th March 1899 that Medmenham Ferry is public.
RIVER THAMES
Farm
1
3

YEWDEN MANOR: Large house which dates from the17th century but has now been split into separate apartments.

GREENLANDS: This sumptuous 19th-century Italianate mansion was once owned by W.H. Smith, the bookseller, publisher and MP. The original house was destroyed by Parliamentary forces in 1644 (cannonballs have since been found) but the present house was rebuilt and extended by Smith after he purchased the estate in 1871. The house is now a management college.

HAMBLEDEN MILL: Impressive weatherboarded mill preserved as residences and worth a quick detour to view from the footpath leading to the lock.

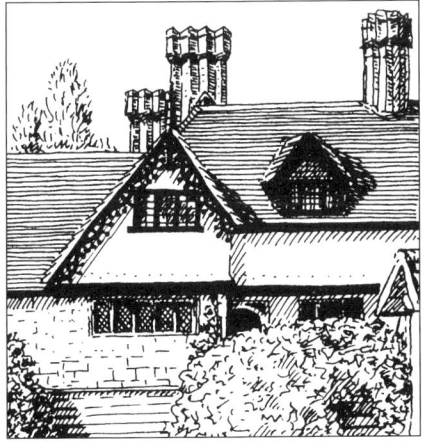

Monks Cottage

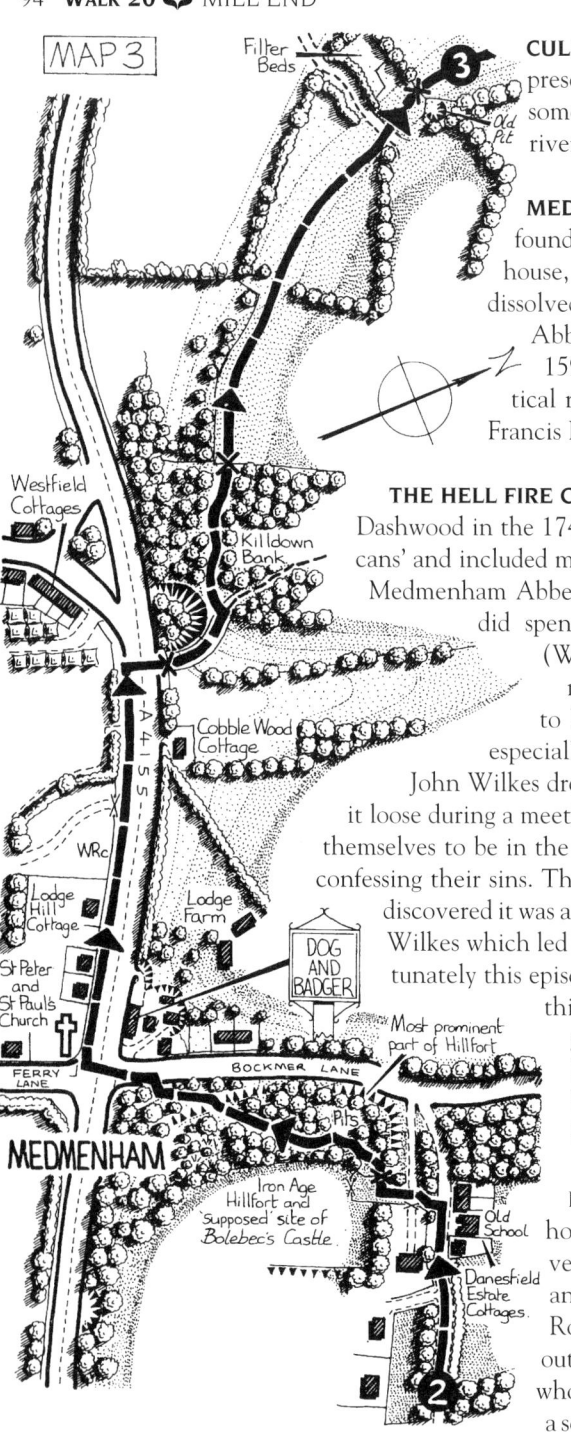

CULHAM COURT: 18th-century house presenting a symmetrical front above some grand steps leading down to the river.

MEDMENHAM ABBEY: The Abbey was founded in 1204 but was never a large house, having only one monk when it was dissolved in the 1530s. The present so-called Abbey is actually a house dating from 1595, and what appear to be ecclesiastical remains are actually follies built by Francis Dashwood in 1755!

THE HELL FIRE CLUB: This brotherhood founded by Dashwood in the 1740s called themselves 'The Franciscans' and included many leading politicians of the time. Medmenham Abbey was their 'temple' although they did spend some time at West Wycombe (Walk 12). Their reputation and later nickname 'The Hell Fire Club' seem to have come as the group fell apart, especially after one famous event in 1763. John Wilkes dressed a baboon as the Devil and let it loose during a meeting. The fellow members, believing themselves to be in the presence of Satan, fell to the floor confessing their sins. Their fear turned to anger when they discovered it was a practical joke and they later framed Wilkes which led to him leaving the country. Unfortunately this episode had focused the public's eye on this secret club and after wildly exaggerated stories of lewd acts and Devil worshipping the group disbanded. Wilkes later returned and became Lord Mayor of London!

DANESFIELD: Originally a farmhouse called Medlicotts it was converted into a mansion in the 1770s and purchased by the soap giant Robert Hudson in 1898. He rebuilt it out of 'clunch', a hard layer of chalk whose whiteness seems appropriate for a soap manufacturer. The remainder of the old estate was sold to Viscount Devonport whose fight to save the Medmenham Ferry is commemorated by the monument near the Thames.

MEDMENHAM: This ancient site has two Iron Age forts on the surrounding hills and a castle. The latter was built in the confines of one of the former, and was associated with Hugh de Bolebec who granted the land for the Abbey around the same time. There are no remains today of the castle but the banks which formed the older hillfort can be traced.

The village below is strung along Ferry Lane from the river up to the church. St Peter and St Paul's dates from the 13th century although most of what you see is due to the restoration in the 19th century. The Dog and Badger opposite claims a foundation of 1390 and was possibly associated with brewing for the Abbey. The present building dates from the 17th century which is reinforced by the find of a cannonball from the Civil War during restoration.

The village hall behind is the old school from 1830 and is set in a former chalk quarry which adds drama to Lodge Farm perched on the edge above. This 17th-century gabled farmhouse was picked out by the Victorian architect Pugin for note as a 'remarkable specimen of brickwork'.

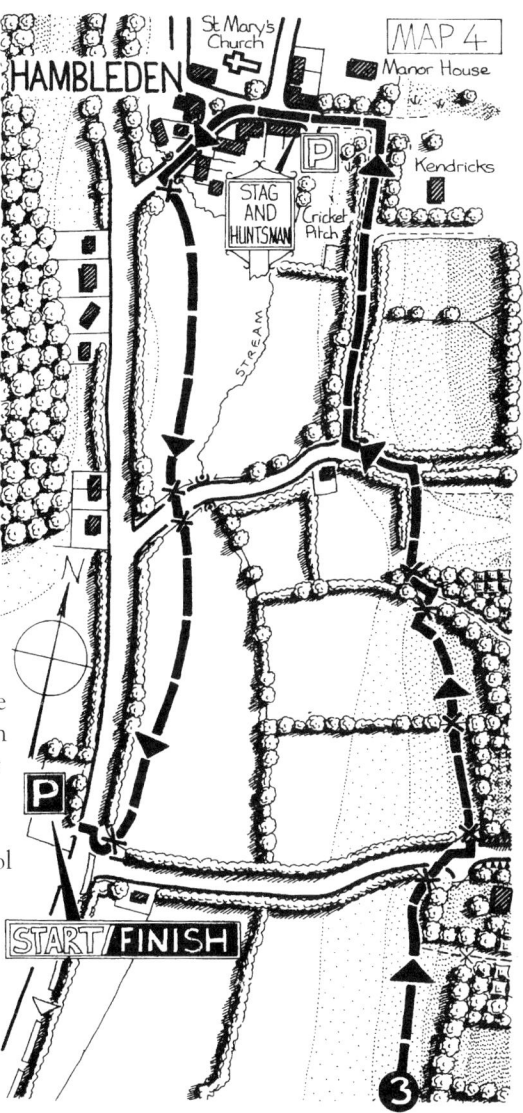

DANESFIELD ESTATE HOUSES: In the village and hidden in the lanes around it are numerous chalky white houses embellished with decoration. These architectural gems were built by Romaine Walker from 1898-1901 in the Arts and Crafts style for Robert Hudson. Look out for the long banks of mullioned windows and the ornate woodwork around the doors and gables.

HAMBLEDEN: Arguably the most picturesque and certainly most photographed village in Buckinghamshire; the haunt of many location film crews and an endless stream of visitors. This continuous flow makes up for the lack of life in the Hamble Stream, a 'winterbourne' which recently hasn't even risen to this modest title. Its inconsistency is well known, having a rep-

Hambledon

a cruciform church and dates back 800 years but was rebuilt only a few centuries later and given a west tower in 1721 after the old central one had collapsed. Inside the tower is panelling with the coat of arms of Cardinal Wolsey which is supposed to have been from his bedstead; while in the churchyard at the rear is the Kendricks Mausoleum.

The Kendricks were responsible for the old Rectory (now Kendricks) which was built around the old Manor House. The present building of that name dates from 1604 and was the birthplace of the Earl of Cardigan who led the famous 'Charge of the Light Brigade' at Balaclava (the cardigan and balaclava were named after this conflict). The remainder of the village consists of cottages – some up to 400 years old – around a triangular area with a Victorian pump.

utation at the turn of the century of flowing for three years then being dry for three more. Despite this in the 1880s it maintained water for nine years allowing the breeding of trout!

At the centre of the village is St Mary's church, another over restored edifice with sharp masonry and grey flints, but attractive thanks to its idyllic setting. It was originally

REFRESHMENTS:

THE DOG AND BADGER, Henley Road, Medmenham. An ancient pub full of character, good beer and food. Open 11 am to 3 pm and 5.30 pm to 11 pm. Telephone: 01491 571362.

THE STAG AND HUNTSMAN, Hambleden. Red-brick pub with bar food and restaurant. Open 11 am to 2.30 pm and 6 pm to 11 pm. Telephone: 01491 571227.

Old Laundry and School House